Peacemaking

Peacemaking

Lance LoRusso

BOOKLOGIX®
Alpharetta, Georgia

10 9 8 7 6 5 4 3 2   1 0 2 8 1 5

ISBN: 978-1-61005-688-5
Library of Congress Control Number: 2015915841

Printed in the United States of America

♾This paper meets the requirements of ANSI/NISO Z39.48-1992 (Permanence of Paper)

DISCLAIMER

This is a work of fiction. Any similarity to persons, places, or entities is purely coincidental. The characters, places, and locations are purely the work of the author's imagination.

Chapter I
Solitude and Solace

He was alone and at peace. It was a different type of peace, deeper than a day off work or spending time reading a good book. It was enveloping, like being relieved of every type of stress in an instant. The kind that comes with a lover's warm embrace, the nuzzle of an old pet, or a child sleeping in your arms. There was no sound, no feeling of warmth or cold, and no sensation of wind or any type of weather. There was, just simply, peace.

Time seemed to stand still, or was it the lack of awareness of time? Losing track of the last events that he clearly remembered, he sat still on the bench, waiting—but for what? Inside his head and heart, he knew he should be here, of that he was certain. He also knew that there was nowhere else he needed to be. It was strange. In a life typically filled with deadlines, schedules, and emergencies, he felt no urgency to know what lay ahead in the next few minutes or the next few hours. Truth be told, the next few years didn't seem to matter. He couldn't remember the last time he had felt that way. Time moved forward for everyone, but for Scotty Painter, time had become irrelevant. He had no idea why, and he had no desire to find out.

Scotty wasn't sure how long he had sat on that bench. It could have been an hour, a day, or a month. He only felt the contentment that comes from a lack of need: no hunger, no thirst, and no anxiety of any kind. He breathed easily and felt the cleanest air enter his lungs. It was intoxicating in a way he had never known.

Many years before, he'd read accounts of people who climbed Everest. They described a feeling of euphoria that separated them from the fatigue of the brutal climb. As the climbers stood at the summit, they told of breathing the thin air like a drug that invigorated them. Scotty often joked with his friends that the climbers were probably describing the effects of taking off their oxygen at 29,000 feet! Whether hypoxia or hyperbole, the descriptions were common among those who had stood at the top of the world.

This feeling was different. Every breath was effortless and comforting. The air was smooth, crisp, and fulfilling. With every cycle in and out, he felt more alive than ever. It reminded him of the relaxation techniques he had learned after his first shooting: "Breathe in through your nose, hold for a count of three, and then breathe out through your mouth." He recalled the words of the department counselor as clear as if she were still sitting next to him. He tried the exercise now, even though there was no stress to "breathe away." Now, there was only solace and peace. A peace he'd never known before, and a peace he'd never imagined.

Although it seemed strange, Scotty hadn't looked around until now. It had never occurred to him to check out his surroundings. This was out of character for a cop. He *always* kept his eyes scanning, looking for exits, threats, and allies. It was the type of habit that made his wife and friends tease him. "Get out of cop mode," they would say. "It's a Fourth of July parade, why can't you just relax?" He had heard it so often that it was now a running joke. Even though he had lived his life this way for years, he just now picked up his head. What he saw was magnificent.

Had he really just looked up, or had his eyes even been open before now? As his mind took in the utter beauty of what he saw, he thought, *My eyes must have been shut! How else could I have missed this?* In front of him and all around was a beauty of nature he had never imagined. Tall mountains, deep blue lakes, and green fields extended as far as he could see. The sky was so rich, saying it was blue seemed inadequate. In the distance, he saw a white sand beach with gentle waves rolling in. He had always been calmed by the ocean. Without a second thought, Scotty stood and began walking through a field toward the waves.

As he walked, he could feel the soft grass beneath his feet. Each step brought him closer to his destination, which at first seemed miles away. Behind him were the white-peaked mountains and, to both sides, beautiful lakes that made him want to dive in. But the ocean was where he wanted to be, where he needed to be. Like a child knows his mother, Scotty just knew he belonged on that beach, close to the waves.

As he walked through the last set of dunes, his senses were filled with the sweet smell of the ocean air. This sensation reminded him of so many vacations to the coast and so many fantastic walks on the beach with his wife, Christine. The beach was where their child, Celina, had taken her first steps and where he had presented her to her groom. The sea was home for him in many ways even though he had never lived near the water. He had felt this way the first time he set foot on a beach as a boy, and it never left his mind.

He thought he was wearing shoes, but he looked down and watched his toes press into the soft white sand. He approached the rolling waves and knew he had arrived. The beach was empty as far as Scotty could see. This was strange. Normally any beach would have someone walking a dog, jogging, or casting into the surf. He'd only seen the beach empty during the dead of winter, his favorite time on the water. However, it was too warm to be wintertime. He couldn't tell how warm or cold it was, just that the weather was perfect. For the first time, he felt an ocean breeze. It felt wonderful, like he could just lean back and float away on it. While he had so many questions about where he was and why, none of that seemed to matter. Scotty just leaned back and took it all in. Any other course of action seemed silly.

Perhaps he would fly away like the gulls and hawks he watched so often. They seemed unchained by the binds of gravity, soaring on thermals, effortlessly moving above the earth and the people who stared at them. How wonderful a feeling, to be so free of tension, struggle, and weighty thoughts as to leave the earth at will. What an amazing view they enjoyed.

Chapter II
You Are Never Alone

He wasn't sure why, but Scotty felt for the first time that he was not alone. It was a strange feeling. Once, on the job, he had felt that way in a dark warehouse when he'd found a broken window while checking a building at night.

"118 to radio."

"Go ahead 118," the operator responded.

"I'm at 2732 Wertz Boulevard off Sammon with a broken window at the rear of the building. Not sure if it is fresh. Possible forced entry. Send another unit."

"10-4."

In a few minutes, two other marked units pulled up with their lights off. One stayed at the front, and one came back to Scotty's location. It was Pete Shona, Scotty's former field training officer.

"What ya got?" Pete said in a whisper.

"Not sure. I've been off for two, but I don't remember this window being out the last time I was back here. What do you think?"

Pete looked at the glass and spoke softly. "It looks fresh to me. See the shards still sticking to the edges? I think we've got us a burglar."

Scotty's stomach tightened as he keyed up his mic. "Radio, hold traffic. Possible Signal 6. Start a keyholder."

The radio volume was turned low now, but Scotty could still hear the operator. "All units hold traffic. 118, 116, and 112 on the scene of a possible Signal 6 at 2732 Wertz Boulevard off Sammon, Boxboard Packaging."

Scotty and Pete pulled the window open slowly. "Are all the doors secure?" Pete asked.

"Unfortunately, yes. I checked every one of them."

"This sucks. I hate window entries. OK. You're in first. I'll cover."

A few minutes later, Pete and Scotty were in the building, moving in a low crouch. It was quiet and the only ambient light came from a few exit signs. Scotty had searched hundreds of buildings by that point in his career, and it never ceased to make his blood burn. He always recalled his academy instructors' warnings: "There are few things more dangerous for a cop than searching a building at night." He was making his way forward with Pete at his back when he felt it. It was hard to describe, but it stopped him in his tracks, and his fingers and toes went cold.

"What's up?" Pete whispered.

"Not sure, but there's someone in here."

Always the joker, Pete whispered, "It's me, bonehead!"

Normally, that comment would have made both of them laugh, but this was different. When Scotty said nothing and just stayed still, Pete knew something was bad wrong. He instantly went serious.

"Radio, I believe we've got one inside," Pete said. He didn't need any further confirmation from Scotty. His job was to have Scotty's back like Scotty had done for him so many times. While he could not hear Radio's response, he knew they would soon have lots of company.

The feeling grew more intense as Scotty listened. Like tracking a wild boar through the woods, tracking bad guys was more than just looking. You had to use your sense of smell and sound and trust your gut. That is what you had to do if you wanted to stay alive.

Then he saw it: a brief change in the shadows in the north corner of the building. There were no trees near the building, and the moon was only half full, so the shadows didn't move much in the tall warehouse.

"North corner, at 11 o'clock," Scotty said.

Pete turned in that direction. "Roger that."

They crept forward slowly to find a man dressed in black wearing a black ski mask. He was crouching behind a trash bin, facing west. Lucky for Scotty and Pete, they approached him from the east. The suspect was looking the other way, waiting for the two uniformed officers—he had a flashlight in one hand and a pistol in the other.

Scotty turned on the weapon light under his M4, and, in that instant, the suspect made the smartest decision of his life. Blinded by Scotty as he turned, he dropped both items, putting his hands in the air. The suspect, a convicted felon, went to jail that night, a place to which he was accustomed.

"Probably looking for the cash box in the office," Pete said later, as they ate breakfast before their shift ended. "What an idiot. Good thing it's illegal for a convicted felon to have a gun," Pete quipped, "otherwise, he might have been armed! Why do they keep letting these guys out? Three felonies, and the last for armed robbery. What did they think he was going to do when he got out on parole, start a flower shop?"

Scotty just shook his head and took another sip of his coffee. He'd been quiet as they ate. "He could have had us if he wanted us."

"Only one of us, my friend! The other would have ended his day."

"True, brother, but I'd prefer he didn't get either one of us!"

"Just another perk of the job, Scotty. We get to meet people who want to kill us with no cover charge. Besides, I'm not worried as long as I have you with me. Jesus, Scotty, you're like a damn psychic! How did you know that guy was in the building? Did you see the shadows move? Is that why you stopped?"

"I saw the shadows move after I knew he was there, Pete. I can't explain it. Maybe I don't want to. I'm just happy we both get to go home tonight with the same amount of holes we started with."

"Amen, brother. You just keep on with your ESP, or ESPN, or whatever it is. You'll never hear me complain."

Scotty felt a change in his awareness like a fog lifting or coming out of a deep sleep. His consciousness of a presence with him on the beach was similar to what he had experienced that night in the warehouse and many times throughout his career. Missing children lost in the woods, senior citizens he had stopped for minor traffic violations driving aimlessly in a bout of dementia, and even felons on car stops that he had approached differently without any real knowledge of the driver's criminal past or evidence that the driver or passengers intended any harm. This was not the same, though. There was no reason for him to expect anyone. While he did not know how long he'd been there, or even where he was, he was sure he was alone. That is, until he felt the presence and heard the voice behind him. The presence was at once calming and familiar.

"It feels great, doesn't it, Scotty?"

Ever the cautious cop, Scotty normally would have spun on his heels to look at the person speaking to him. However, for reasons he could not explain, Scotty did not move.

"What do you mean? Everything feels great right now."

"The air. Clean. Crisp. The scent of the sea. There's nothing like it, is there?"

"I can't argue with that."

"It reminds you of walking with Celina and Christine on East Beach on St. Simons Island, doesn't it?"

"Yes, it does." Scotty was a bit uneasy, but not scared. Normally, a comment like that from a stranger would have put him on the defensive, but he just stood there, relaxed. A part of his brain was fighting to put him on alert, but it caught no traction. Instead, he found himself comforted by the words.

"I miss that time in my life," Scotty volunteered. "Life was simpler then—calm."

"I know. That's why you're here. It's important for you to know that good feelings, good times, and tranquility await you."

"Maybe for some people, but not for me. Too many bills, too many victims, too many perps on the street who will keep hurting people if we don't catch them."

"You said 'we' Scotty. Don't you mean you?"

"Me, them, what's the difference? Someone's gotta go get them. It's rarely just one of us. It takes all of us."

"It does take a lot of people to keep others safe, Scotty, and doing so is honorable. However, it doesn't always have to be you."

Those words hit home. Scotty had been a cop for nearly thirty years now. He had turned down promotions and assignments to stay in homicide for nearly ten of those years, then he finally started moving up the ranks. All of his assignments required teamwork, but he was always a part of that team. He dreaded the day he would be forced to retire. He knew the work would go on without him, but he couldn't bear the thought of not contributing to the effort. How could this person say this? This was one of his most deeply held beliefs. How did this stranger know that?

"I know, Scotty, because I know all there is to know about you. Even the hairs on your head have been counted."

On these words, Scotty slowly turned. It was obvious that the voice knew what he was thinking. Even though the question never passed his lips, the answer came from the voice behind him. Scotty fully turned behind him to see the source of the voice. As his eyes took in the sight before him, and his brain struggled to comprehend what he saw, the peace Scotty had felt upon first opening his eyes in this place returned. His mind slowly formed the thought that he had heard expressed in words, but that had always seemed inadequate in the past. *Behold the majesty of the Lord.*

Chapter III
As a Shepherd for His Flock

The figure before Scotty was instantly familiar. As a cop, he was legendary with faces, once recognizing a wanted fugitive in a news camera shot of a crowd. However, he could not place the man. Scotty studied his face, mannerisms, and body language but received no triggers for his memory. Not only did the man look familiar, his presence made Scotty comfortable. He was a white man in his late fifties. He was dressed about the way Scotty would dress on his days off. His haircut and color were about the same as Scotty's, and he was the same height and build.

"Take your time, Scotty. There's no rush. However, I can tell you we met a long time ago. I looked different back then; so did you."

"Tell me about it, but that doesn't help. It seems I looked different last month. Did you have dark hair the last time we met?

"Of course, Scotty, and so did you."

"Were you a cop?" Scotty began to stare intently, looking for a subtle clue from this stranger's face.

"Well, that's hard to answer. I will say we're in the same business. You watch over the public, and I watch over you and your brother and sister officers." The stranger paused and took a deep breath. "I watch over everyone."

"What do you mean, you watch over me and my brother and sister officers?"

"You've heard this many times. You knew this from the time you were a small boy. You've heard the words thousands of times in many venues."

"What words?" Scotty's mind was starting to race. He was not accustomed to being off-balance like this.

"Blessed are the peacemakers."

Scotty stood frozen. The words held him in a grip so tight that he could not move yet so comforting that he felt like he had waited for this feeling his whole life. He'd heard this Bible passage at every law enforcement funeral and every church service during National Police Week in Washington, DC. Every time he heard it, he remembered what he had learned in Sunday school. The teachers told him that peacemakers were servants of God who put their safety second to the well-being of others. No one else knew how those words had inspired him and comforted him throughout his life. In that instant, Scotty knew the identity of the stranger who stood before him and embraced that recognition with every ounce of his being.

"How can that be? You look so ordinary, so common."
Part of Scotty still wanted to question what he was hearing, while a part of him deeply wanted it to be true.

"Far from common, Scotty, I look familiar to you because this is an appearance that comforts you. No person
is common. Everyone is unique. They are unique in the
way they look, feel, think, act, and believe. That is the only
way they would have the ability to make the choices that
make up their lives."

"But they make bad choices. Many do bad and horrific
things," Scotty said, nearly choking up. "Why would you
let that happen?"

"It happens, Scotty, because I am not a puppet master.
I am the giver of life and also the giver of choice. While
I know the path that lies ahead for every man, woman,
and child, it is a path of their choosing."

"So what is the choice? If their paths will lead to murder, rape, and destruction, what choices do they have?"

"They all have the choice to find the strength within
them to change, Scotty. Everyone has the ability to put
their life on a different and better track. However, I cannot
make them do so. One day, they will answer for those
choices, but I only provide them the tools they need and
the opportunities to make good choices. The rest is up to
them."

Scotty hung his head down. He felt exhausted. He
sat down on the sand and took a deep breath. He was

overwhelmed with emotion. After catching his breath, he felt the need to speak. However, his words seemed inadequate. How could he ask? Why wasn't his faith strong enough to definitively answer the question for him? Why was he still hanging onto the doubt in his mind when his heart knew the truth? Would speaking the words demonstrate a lack of faith, or merely his mortal limitations?

Scotty kept his head down and stared at the sand as he spoke. "I have two questions."

"You have many questions, Scotty."

"Yes, but let's start with these two. Why am I here?"

"Your choices brought you here, Scotty. There is no other place for you to be at this time."

Scotty thought hard about the next question. As the words passed from his brain to his lips, he could hardly believe he was speaking them. He slowly lifted his head and swallowed hard. As tears began to fill his eyes, he spoke the words that at once seemed to betray his faith and also confirm it. "Are you my God?"

The stranger standing on the sand looked deeply into Scotty's eyes. In any other context, it would have seemed like an uncomfortable stare, but now, in this moment, it was more akin to a powerful embrace. "I am the light, the truth, and the way, Scotty. I am the father who cared for you every second that you experienced life's struggles. I am your biggest supporter. I took joy in your triumphs and wept with you in your lows. I pulled you from the brink of darkness when tragedy struck your family and gave you the strength to continue on your journey. I am your God, Scotty, by whatever name I am called. I am Christ, your savior."

The words seemed to strike deep in Scotty's heart, lifting all the burdens he had carried from the time he was a boy. Scotty's body felt heavy, but his mind had never been clearer. He looked up at the figure before him and saw clearly, even though the sun was strong. Scotty lay down on the soft sand and took in a few deep breaths of the clean salt air. As his eyes closed, he tried to fight the slumber that fell upon him.

"So many questions." His words were soft and barely audible.

"Sleep, my son. Rest and know that I am with you. I will be here when you awaken, as I have always been every day of your life."

Scotty's last image of the man before him was watching him sit on the sand, take a deep breath, and begin to stare at the sea. Scotty faded off into an effortless sleep as the words echoed in his head. "I will be here when you awaken, as I have always been every day of your life."

Chapter IV
Answers without Questions and Questions without Answers

Scotty woke to the soft sounds of the sea. Gulls were chasing each other, the waves were slowly rising to the sand, and the soft, warm breezes embraced his body. He opened his eyes to see the glory before him. Scotty had felt this way a thousand times while hunting when the sun rose, the warmth striking his body and the woods awakening to a new day.

"It's not easy, you know," Christ said as he sat on the sand. Just as Scotty did when he went to the beach, he was tossing small pebbles into the surf.

"What's not easy?"

"Watching people make bad choices. Seeing them hurt themselves and each other. So much unnecessary sadness and pain."

Scotty thought for a moment about what he heard. He had never considered the anguish of a loving God looking down on his children, only to feel pain and disappointment at the way they lived.

"Could you change them?" Scotty was surprised how easily the question came to his lips. He was not hesitating as he had before.

"When I walked on Earth, I fed thousands with five loaves and two fishes. I brought sight to a blind man. I raised a child from the dead. All things are possible through me, Scotty."

Scotty thought about Christ's response. "If you can intervene, why not do so? Why not get into the heart of the rapists, terrorists, and serial killers and change them?"

Christ smiled. "You have lived your life as a man of action, Scotty. You receive a call for help or see a crisis, and you respond. That is your world and the world of your brothers and sisters in uniform. You act from a sense of duty."

"But you act out of love."

"Love and understanding, Scotty. There is a place for suffering in the world, Scotty. Many times, suffering brings joy, satisfaction, and change. You must remember that I also have so much joy watching my children. I see them experience happiness at their successes. I watch them beam with pride and love when their children succeed. I see the triumph of the challenged athlete at the Special Olympics, the musician who masters a classical performance before a packed hall, and the scientific breakthrough of the woman who finally isolated the gene that causes all cancers. I see all of that."

Christ continued as Scotty looked on, "I also see the poor who help each other, the rich man who secretly gives to strangers, and the people who sacrifice every day to enrich the lives of others. How fortunate I am to be able to witness the good choices made by so many millions of my children."

Scotty thought about this response. Was it really an answer? The detective in him wanted to push harder, but he felt his discomfort stemmed more from the fact that he just didn't understand the answer.

"You said it is not easy watching them make bad choices. Is it enough for you to see the good? Is that what carries you through?" Scotty hoped his question made sense.

"You have always had a keen sense of things, Scotty. I remember when you were a boy, you wondered out loud why people would hurt children when you saw a news story of some men who stole a bus filled with children and held them in the desert."

The statement triggered a memory for Scotty. He was only nine or ten years old at the time. It was a national news event. The children were all found safe in a buried trailer.

Jesus spoke again. "It is always enough for me, as it must be. The gift our Father gave mankind was the opportunity to live life. What could be more precious?"

"But He has been angered in the past."

"Of course. Like every parent, He has been angered and disappointed. He has also been warmed by the love shown by His children and their great accomplishments. You see, the good and the bad are part of life. When there is one, there will always be the other as long as people have free will. Without free will, people would not be alive. A gracious and loving God can give no more than the freedom to make one's life into what it will be. Do you understand, Scotty?"

There was a long pause as Scotty reflected on his question. Could anyone really understand this? Scotty felt like he had somehow just now peeked through a small window into a vast room. As he thought about what to say, he was finally at ease with both the time it was taking for him to ask and his next question itself.

"How do you deal with the pain?" Scotty said quietly, staring back down at the sand.

"Why do you ask?"

"There is no caring without pain at what you described. If you love so deeply, there will be suffering for you in watching the suffering of others. Just as the joy of others brings you joy, so must their sadness affect you."

"You know me better than you think, Scotty." Christ paused and took a deep breath. He looked away from Scotty towards the slow, rolling waves. "Yes, I feel pain and so does our Father. When I learned of the death of John the Baptist, I was in pain. I left to be alone, but when the people followed me, I was lifted by their faith. So it is every day, Scotty. Every second of what you know as every day, there is so much good to fill and lift me. When there is sadness, tragedy, and evil, I rely on the promise of the coming good and peace to pull me through to the next second. It is for me as I told you, 'Let not your hearts be troubled.' As you trust in me, I trust in the Father. What further comfort could I need?"

Scotty pondered the words. He wondered all his life how evil was permitted to exist. Not only exist, but it seemed to thrive in his world. As an officer, the tragic circumstances of life were more than headlines; they were vivid memories burned into the mind and soul, never to be forgotten. In a strange way, Christ's answer seemed to be enough for him. It was not a revelation, as he expected one day to receive. It was more an understanding of why the world was, well, as it was.

Scotty lifted his head and again looked at Christ. "Was it harder to walk among us as a man, or to watch now from above?"

"Not harder. Different, I suppose, but you know the difference from your own life."

The words humbled Scotty. "How could I possibly have experienced anything close to that?"

"Think back on your promotion to major. Do you remember?"

Scotty's mind wandered to a vivid memory of cleaning out his office when he was a captain in the intelligence and drug squad. It was quite an undertaking as he removed diplomas and plaques from the wall and boxed up the knickknacks that had inexplicably multiplied over his career. One of his sergeants came in and sat down. His open-door policy had led to many such impromptu visits.

"We're gonna miss you around here, sir." John Downing was a hulk of a man who could clean up to look like a recruiting poster in uniform, or dress down and sell meth to any dealer. Scotty respected him a lot.

"You'll manage without me. Besides, you folks will have your hands full breaking in a new captain." Both men laughed.

"I'm going to miss this, John. I like being on the street with the troops, being in the action, and sharing the highs and lows."

"I'm sure you will, but we need you in the control tower." This was a term used by the rank and file to refer to the chief's office and all associated administrative positions. The name came from a previous chief who had always seemed to be watching everyone from the clouds, looking for someone to mess up. Although the new chief was very different, the nickname had stuck, like many others in the law enforcement world.

"It'll be a challenge. I just hope I can make a difference by making the big decisions. It seems like it will be a lot harder looking down and making judgment calls rather than being in the thick of it."

"I totally disagree! Most folks can't handle the job on the street. Then they get into the control tower and make decisions that have no foundation in reality. You will have the benefit of a lot of years in the trenches listening to the cops doing the job. Scotty Painter will never forget where he came from." The words were the best compliment Scotty could hope for.

"Thanks, John, but it's the folks doing the job I'm concerned about, and I always have been. Have we done enough to train them? Have we selected the right candidates? Do they have the courage to do their jobs? Will they falter when they're faced with danger?"

"After years on the road and in training, Captain, you know they do. You also know in many cases they have you to thank for it. That includes me." The two men looked at each other. No further words needed to be spoken about the incident that had nearly ended John's career years earlier when a hostage-taker had made good on his promise to kill.

"We're buying you dinner tonight at Rocco's. No excuses."

"No arguments here!" The two men shook hands. "I hope you knuckleheads don't have anything big planned for dinner."

"Well, it's always good to be hopeful." John smiled and left Scotty's office.

As Scotty reflected on the memory, Christ spoke again. "He was right, Scotty. You never forgot what mattered to you. So it is for me. I cherish every day I walked on Earth. The richness of the human experience cannot be overstated."

"Many of the days you spent on Earth were horrible, and you knew all things before you were born. You knew what you were facing."

"I wouldn't say 'horrible' so much as 'busy'; I had a lot to accomplish." Christ smiled and winked at Scotty. The two men looked at each other for a moment. In that time, Scotty began to understand that Christ viewed his persecution as work to be done on Earth: a labor of love. "You didn't want to leave the 'thick of it' because you were afraid that you would lose touch with what really mattered, but that never happened. You held on to those memories and experiences, and they made you a better person. They also made you a better sheepdog keeping the wolves away from your officers."

"I'd like to think I helped." Scotty blinked several times to stop his eyes from filling with tears. With every officer injured or killed, he always wondered if he had done enough.

"You did, Scotty. This may seem simple, but I would not have truly been the Son of God if I had not spent time on Earth with His children. We all learn not only from our mistakes but from the mistakes and triumphs of others."

Scotty thought about those words. That was his goal: to be an example to others and learn from everyone he met. To hear for even a moment that he'd succeeded was a bit overwhelming.

"Sounds like you need more convincing." Christ smiled.

Scotty looked up at Christ. "Sorry, but it's a hard thing to be sure of. I mean, in the moment of doing the right thing, you can never be sure."

"You never focused on the results, Scotty, and that's what's most important. You did the right thing . . . " Christ let his voice trail off.

"'Cause it was the right thing to do. You've heard me say that many times."

"Yes, I have." Christ looked up toward the beautiful blue sky. "And you made us proud every time you said it."

Christ looked back at Scotty, and the two sat in silence. Just then a name entered Scotty's mind: Reggie Pelletier.

Scotty's mind drifted to a dark time in his memories. He was back in his office as a major over operations. He had just returned from the scene of a shooting involving one of his officers, a new officer with about two years on the street. Scotty hated those calls. He always prayed the officer would survive, but he also knew that if the officer was forced to take a life to survive, a family somewhere would be grieving. That day, the officer survived. Reggie Pelletier would see the sunrise the following morning. The suspect would not.

As Scotty settled into his chair, his cell phone rang.

"Painter," he answered.

"Major, sorry to bother you, it's Officer Pelletier. Do you have a second, sir?"

"Of course, Reg. What's up? Are you OK?" Scotty knew his nickname. He knew every officer under his command. They were his responsibility, his charges, and as he got more gray on his head, they seemed more like his children.

"You said I could call you any time, but if I need to go through my chain of command, I will. I mean, I don't want to get in trouble or cause any problems, but—"

Scotty cut him off. "Take a breath, Reg. What's on your mind?"

"It's just hard, sir. I mean, I killed somebody's mother." Pelletier burst into tears.

"Where are you, Reg?"

"Mountain Park, at the top."

"Stay put. I'm on the way."

"I'll be OK, sir, and you have other things to do."

"I have nothing more important to do than speak with you, Reg. Sit tight."

Scotty left his office and covered the four miles to the city park in about five minutes. Mountain Park was the pride of the city. It was a huge park that served as the site of community gatherings, fundraisers, and the start and finish of the annual Run for the Blue 5K to raise money for Hunting for Heroes and Concerns of Police Survivors. Scotty was worried until he remembered why this place had significance for Reggie; he'd won the 5K last spring. On that day, he was honored for his fitness and dedication to his community. Today he returned to find reassurance that he was still one of the good guys.

Scotty found Reggie on a rock, looking over the city toward the river. He was hunched over and sobbing. It was a stark contrast to the confident man Scotty saw in uniform every day. Scotty approached and stood behind him. He thought of what to say for some time, then he remembered a comment he'd heard from a person in mourning. "It doesn't matter what people say during those times; it matters that they are there." Scotty put his right hand on Reggie's left shoulder and squeezed.

"It wasn't supposed to be a woman."

"I know, Reg."

"I prepared myself that I might have to take a life one day to save myself, another officer, or some kid being held hostage. I was ready for that day." He paused to get his breath. "In every scenario, even my dreams, the bad guy was always a guy. Sometimes he was tall or short, armed with probably every type of weapon imaginable, committing a variety of crimes . . . " His voice trailed off.

"It's OK, Reg. Keep talking."

After a few minutes, Reggie controlled his breathing enough to begin speaking again.

"Even in my dreams—more like nightmares—when I was being choked out, or couldn't get my gun out, I saw the bad guy as a guy, you know? But she was shooting at us! I told her to stop, to put the gun down. I probably hesitated too long. We could have been killed because I hesitated."

Scotty closed his eyes. The grief surrounding this young officer was palpable. "But you weren't killed. You acted. You turned your fear into action. Reggie, you saved your partner and that cashier. I've seen the surveillance video. What may have seemed like a lifetime of hesitation was in reality only a split second."

"I know, but I killed a woman! What kind of a man does that make me?" Reggie collapsed into his own hands as he sobbed with abandon. They were the sobs of a child in a man's body. Inconsolable. Raw emotion. Pain leaving the body through tears expressed as agony. Scotty knew words were inadequate now. He sat down next to Reggie and put his right arm around him. He held him tight. He made up his mind: he would stay there all night if he had to. Both men sat there as the sun began to set and the sky turned bright with beautiful colors. It was only then that they began speaking again. The sorrow gone, the confident man returning, Scotty could speak with Reggie and help him.

"Let's move around a bit." As they walked to their cars, Reggie shook Scotty's hand.

"Thanks, Chief."

"Chief? I'm a major! Have your eyes gotten so swollen that you can't see the oak leaves?"

"No, sir. I see the rank. The leader of any department is the chief and you are a true leader. I'll never forget your support."

"I'm honored that you called me, Reg."

"I knew you had been through it, you know. Dropped a hammer and nearly died."

The reference made Scotty's gut tighten as it always did. "I learned a lot living with those memories, Reg. I shot that man in front of his children." Scotty paused and choked back a crack in his voice that he could sense was coming.

"It still affects you? How long ago was that?"

"Fifteen years this October." Scotty realized his head had dropped and he was looking down. He took a deep breath and picked up his head, looking Reggie in the eyes. "For a long time, I just worked to try not to think about it every day. That was my goal—hoping and knowing that day would come."

"How long did that take?"

"Ten years."

"Wow." Reggie stared at Scotty without realizing it.

Scotty had seen that stare before and broke the uncomfortable silence. "You'll get there, Reg. Just don't rush it."

"I hope I do. That seems like a long time, though."

"For a cop, Reg, doing your job often means taking on everyone else's burdens. We do the stuff no one else wants to do, and worse, we handle the problems no one else wants to admit exists."

"*Ego pugna malum vos precor does nusquam esse,*" Reggie said effortlessly.

"I fight the evil you pray does not exist." Scotty's quick reply surprised Reggie.

"I have a medallion that says that. I guess it is even more true with my shooting."

"It is part of your life now, Reg, but it's a good life. You are a good man who risked his life to protect others. Don't forget that in the next few days."

"Yes, sir."

"I want you to remember something else."

"What's that?"

"My cell number. 24/7, Reg. Just call."

The two men got into their cars and left the park. Commander and officer, on an equal plane for a brief period, now returning to their respective roles.

Scotty's last memory of Reggie was the photo he received of Reggie graduating from the FBI Academy three years later. He signed the photo with an inscription, "To Chief Painter, *Vos operor non pugna unus*. Reg." Scotty had a tough time explaining that inscription to the real chief, but he treasured that photo.

"You do not fight alone," Christ said and smiled.

"Yes," Scotty replied and just accepted the fact that he hadn't spoken the words aloud. Christ was living the memory with him.

"Are you convinced now, Scotty? You see, people don't need to move mountains to change the world. If you needed that ability, our Father would have given you that strength. You only need to have the courage to act and the compassion to reach out to others."

"You sold me!" Scotty smiled.

Christ smiled back and laughed. "Well, Scotty, I have been known to turn a phrase and have been told I can be quite convincing."

Time passed slowly in a place with no measure of time. Scotty was sitting up now, next to Christ, as both tossed pebbles into the waves. They were like small children sitting side by side without a care in the world. Scotty chuckled as he likened them to Charlie Brown and Linus on the wall at the end of an episode. At that very instant, Christ chuckled as well.

"I've always been fascinated by the ocean waves. They seem endless. We toss these pebbles into the surf, and in time, they will be here again, exactly where we found them." As he spoke, Scotty looked around at the millions of pebbles mixed in with the soft sand on the beach.

"And they are all unique. Have you ever pondered that?" Christ said. "Take a handful and look at them."

Scotty grabbed a big handful of pebbles and sand. He was about to say that he didn't have his glasses when he looked down and saw, more clearly than ever, the details of each. It was nothing he could ever remember seeing: each ridge, crystal, and edge. It was true. Each was unique and beautiful.

"So it is with people, Scotty. Each has different characteristics. People mostly see the visible differences of skin, eye, and hair color. They may notice a different shape of a face. With a few people throughout their lives, they are fortunate enough to see the things inside that make them unique: their talents, their analysis of what goes on around them, or their wisdom in guiding themselves and others. Whatever the qualities, good and bad, that make them unique, how privileged I am to know it all for every person!"

"There was a man," Scotty said. "I met him when I was a rookie. He took a child hostage and threatened to cut the boy's throat with a knife. I watched that man for hours, it seemed. I could see his face, his eyes, his expressions, and I heard his words. I nearly ended his life, but I never knew him. I also never understood why he would hurt a child that he lived with, his girlfriend's son."

"I stood with you that night, Scotty. Just as I was disappointed with that man, I was proud of you and your beat partner. I guided your hand as you pulled that trigger and stopped it as he dropped the knife at the last second."

Scotty thought back to that night, and his memory was as vivid as ever. He saw the dingy walls of the cheap apartment, the stained carpet, and the nasty chair the man sat in with the child on his lap. In his left hand, he supported the three-year-old child. In his right, he held a butcher knife to the boy's throat. This memory had come to Scotty many times after that night. It awakened him, brought him out of the escape of many movies, and always seemed to make his heart race. If he was dreaming, it ended many ways—sometimes with the man's head splattered on the wall after a shot from Scotty's revolver, and sometimes, the boy did not survive the first movement of the big knife. This time, although the memory was clearer than ever, Scotty was calm.

"I understand now why you did not stop him from taking the child hostage, but I still do not understand why anyone would do something so cruel. There are so many other people I've encountered. There were also people in the news. They killed women and children and tortured innocent people. Bad choices are one thing, but why were they so cruel?"

"There is a capability of every man and woman to be gracious and selfish, to be compassionate and cruel, to forgive and to condemn."

A natural silence seemed to follow. It was as if they were old friends, just passing the time.

"I can accept that." The words seemed more a thought than a sentence. As Scotty said them, he realized that he did not hear anything. Then he wondered had he even spoken at all to Christ, or were they communicating without words?

"I felt your presence before." The words seemed almost like Scotty spoke them in a different language. His body seemed moved by each word he spoke.

"I'm glad, Scotty. I was always there for you."

"No." The word seemed too harsh. "I mean, really, I felt you there." Scotty was nearly trembling as he struggled to speak.

"When?" Christ looked at Scotty and put his hand on Scotty's shoulder.

Scotty took a moment to gather the words to describe the memory he was forming in his mind. It was a memory he had discarded long ago. "I was a little boy, the night my father died. I was in my room. No one would come upstairs because they thought I was asleep, but I knew something was going on."

"Tell me what you remember."

"The house was always quiet at night, even when my dad was working. When he came home, he barely made any noise, but I tried to stay up. It was easier to sleep when I knew he was home for the night. That night, I went to bed and drifted off, but something woke me up. After I was awake, I heard voices, strange voices, and one familiar one."

"Who was it?"

"Our pastor, Pastor Joe. He had a calm but deep voice. You could hear it in the basement of the church from one end to the other. He was such a good man and loved kids."

"Do you remember anything he said?"

"It was hard to hear because I was upstairs, but I heard him ask if I was asleep. Then he and the other person went into the kitchen with my mom. They talked for a long time. I heard something about a car, and I heard her cry. I just knew something was wrong with my dad."

"You were alone and scared, Scotty."

"I was scared, but I was not alone. When you came to me on the beach, I knew your presence was familiar, but I did not know why. Now I remember. As I waited for someone to come upstairs, I thought about going down to check on my mom, but I was too scared to move. I guess I didn't want to know what they were talking about because I had a feeling it was very bad. So I started praying."

"Yes, you did. You prayed the pure and simple words of a child."

"I felt silly sometimes doing it. Many of my friends didn't understand, and they made fun of me. Even the kids I knew from Sunday school got weird when I prayed about something. As I got older, I learned to pray quietly to myself, but that night, I prayed out loud."

"You said, 'Father, please take care of my mom and me. We still need my daddy, but I understand you may need him more. I won't be mad at you if you called him home with Grandpa and Granny, I promise. But I'm scared.' I remember those words, Scotty."

Scotty looked down. It was amazing that he was hearing again the words he'd so innocently spoken as a child. The memory brought him close to that little boy that he was so many years ago. He felt small and helpless again as he did that night.

"You were there. I felt it, but I never told anyone, ever."

"Why not, Scotty?"

"I thought it would scare my mom. Pastor Joe stayed with me, and the other person drove her away. She came back after daylight and told me he was gone. I'll never forget that morning. I had to be strong for her." Scotty paused. "Besides, I didn't know what to say."

"You needed me, Scotty. I've been there for and with you many times, but that night, you needed me next to you."

"Why me? With all the other kids in the world who were hungry, in pain, and in danger, why me?" Scotty had wondered all these years if Christ was really with him that night. As he learned that it was true, he did not understand how he was worthy of such attention.

"Prayers are a funny thing, Scotty. People pray for everything from forgiveness to the winning lottery numbers." Christ smiled and Scotty took a deep breath. "Sometimes, people pray out of desperation and other times out of need. My Father and I hear them all, but let's just say some of them hit home harder than others."

"How long did you stay with me?"

"I hugged you and watched you fall asleep. I stayed until Pastor Joe woke you to feed you breakfast."

Scotty stared blankly up at the sky. He took a deep breath and spoke.

"Thank you." The words seemed to fall out of his mouth. Then he could not speak. He was overwhelmed with emotion.

Christ put his hand on Scotty's shoulder. Neither of them spoke for a long time.

"I kept praying. It was hard losing my dad, and I needed to pray."

"I know, Scotty. It was a great arrangement: You kept praying and I kept listening." Christ smiled.

Scotty felt tired. Just as he relaxed, a sharp pain ripped into him, and he arched his back. Burning, tearing. It seemed like he would never escape the agony. The pain seemed real. Was it worse because he had been so calm in the instant prior? Just when he believed he could take no more, the pain was gone. Scotty was lying on his back looking up, and Christ was smiling at him.

Chapter V
So As You Do to Each Other

He had never seen a more radiant smile. Christine was in her element—laughing, hugging, and just living life. She walked up to Scotty and put her arm around him.

"How awesome is this? Everyone together having fun! How does it feel to be an old man?"

Scotty smiled and looked around. Although he did not feel old, that was apparently not the consensus of the group assembled. Signs reading "Caution: Old Fart Working" and "Old Age and Treachery Will Win Over Youth Every Time!" adorned the Fraternal Order of Police Lodge where Scotty and about a hundred people had gathered to celebrate his fiftieth birthday. Although Scotty would not admit it, only one sign made him truly chuckle: "I believe in the hereafter . . . it seems closer every day!"

Christine and a few of Scotty's closest friends had organized the event. Celina was there with her husband. She seemed so happy. It was only a few months ago that he walked her down the aisle and gave her away.

Peter was a good man, not a kid, as he'd heard so many dads say when they watched their daughters marry. Peter was a man, and his little girl deserved nothing less. As he formed this thought, he had to chuckle. *Funny how we always see the world through our own lens,* he thought.

Bob Shoop, the chief of police, was there. He and Scotty had known each other since the academy. They were more than friends. It was a bond formed through good times with their families, celebrating promotions, standing over the recently departed as homicide detectives, and attending funerals for officers. It was unbreakable. Blood and lineage aside, they were brothers.

The chief gathered everyone's attention, then spoke. "So, it's true and official! Scotty Painter is not as old as everyone thought he was!"

As usual, Bob's words caused the crowd to erupt into laughter. Even Scotty had to laugh.

"I want to say a few words about this guy. When we hear the words 'he's a cop's cop' my mind goes to one face—Scotty Painter. If he worked for you, he made you look good. If you worked for him, he had your back, and if you worked with him, you probably spent the day laughing your ass off!"

That last bit caused the crowd to erupt in laughter again. Spontaneous cheers of "Here, here!" echoed.

"When I was asked to come and speak today, I thought carefully about this event. Scotty turning fifty! How could I let that opportunity pass? Then I thought about the management gurus who say you should never drink alcohol and celebrate with your troops. Of course, in the end, it came down to this: There would be free food, and Christine would be here, so it was a no-brainer!"

The applause was thundering! As Scotty looked at Christine, she was red-faced and embarrassed. Scotty had grown accustomed to such comments, as well as Christine's reaction. It was undeniable, though. She was a strikingly beautiful woman.

"I want to propose a toast to one of the best cops I know, my friend, mentor, confidant, and brother. Scotty Painter is a part of the bedrock of this department like the bricks that form the base of our headquarters and the hearts that drive our officers. May his life be long, his career fulfilling, and his retirement, if he EVER retires, be long and gratifying!" He paused for the applause. "Until that day, we feel privileged and honored for each day he chooses to work with us. God bless you and your family, my friend. Here's to fifty more—or as many as you want!"

Scotty looked around at the crowd as they all toasted him. Christine held him tight. "Do you want to say something, Scotty?"

"In a few. I don't think I can talk right now." Scotty squeezed her and kissed her lips.

Christ's words seemed to peacefully transition Scotty from that pleasant memory back to the beach. "What a great memory!"

"It's always been hard for me to listen to that type of speech. I know others always deserve it more than I do," Scotty said.

"Perhaps, but that doesn't change the fact that you are deserving of such praise."

"I don't know. How many times was I selfish with my time? How many opportunities did I let pass me by? How many more people could have benefitted from my efforts, however small they might have been?"

Christ seemed to ponder these questions. It was the first time that Scotty saw him thinking about an answer.

"'Go and serve the Lord.' How many times have you heard that, Scotty?"

"I couldn't even count. Every time I went to church. Thousands."

"That's right. That was all I asked of my apostles and the people of the world. That means different things to different people, and I understand that. For some, that means giving up their worldly possessions to serve in the clergy, and for others it means lending their talents to their church. That's OK, Scotty. You see, people serve the Lord by living their lives. More than that, Scotty, they serve by not living their lives in fear or wasting the life they've been given."

These were powerful words that struck at the core of Scotty Painter. He thought of the people he had met throughout his life who walked in fear every day. He remembered people unwilling to change their circumstances and seek an education or do something to better their chance at a better life. The business people that he stopped for speeding drove nice cars and wore beautiful clothes, but they were too busy rushing around to realize they had a good life. He also thought of the people who did give up everything to serve others. There were so many but, at the same time, not enough considering how many people were in need.

"So, the command is not to stop living your life. You want people to serve you by living their lives to the fullest while helping others to do so?"

"Yes, Scotty. However, 'Go and serve the Lord' is not a command. It is a wish, a desire. It is the hope and dream of a loving Father. In other words, you will have an opportunity to see the sun on your face tomorrow. What you choose to do with the day you've been given is your choice. But as you make those choices, be guided by the understanding of the awesome gift each day truly is."

"And what of the people who do nothing for others? Who live selfishly, thinking only of their own needs and desires? Will they be judged harshly?"

Christ turned to look directly at Scotty. His face was warm and open like a parent trying to explain something complicated to a small child, yet at the same time filled with compassion for the internal struggle raised by the question.

"There are so many ways to the same destination. Some get lost, Scotty. Some never lose their way. Others seem to never understand where they are headed. How can a loving God turn His back on His children? Just as you were disappointed when Celina was caught drinking underage and were angry that she had made a bad choice that could have ended or changed the course of her life, I sometimes shake my head and ache with the choices made by my children. But I never stop loving them." Christ paused. "I never stop cheering them on and hoping that every day will bring them closer to happiness. Judgment is a complicated thing. Our Father sent me to take your sins so that you would be forgiven. The daily missteps of people in their daily lives are not sins, Scotty. They are, at best, brief lapses and, at worst, stumbles along their journey."

Scotty was sure he looked a bit confused, although he had always believed that the Father could rarely condemn His children. He'd read the Bible verses and listened with skepticism to sermons that played up the notion that one misstep in life could send a person tumbling into eternal damnation. How wonderful it was to hear that his thoughts of a merciful God were correct.

"In your own life, Scotty, how many people have you seen turn their lives around? I remember a woman with three children living in an abusive relationship who turned her awful life into a meaningful one after she met you. Do you remember her? She did horrible things while living in the lowest valleys of despair. She now stands tall on the mountains of her life. She is living the life intended for her; one of rich fulfillment. The same is true for those children she raised to not live in fear despite their surroundings. That is what to 'serve the Lord' means, Scotty. Although she never spent a day in a church, her love of God is strong in her heart and nothing can hide that. She shows that love in her words and deeds every day."

Scotty remembered the woman and her children. Tanya Ronder had no hope when Scotty met her that Friday night. She was beaten and bruised. She lay on her side, unconscious after making a last effort to protect the fragile bodies of her children. When Scotty responded to the 911 call with two other officers, he was the first to enter the trailer, and he immediately crashed through the rotted floor. He saw Tanya on the floor to his left and her husband, Jay Adrian Sanda, to his right. Every cop in the precinct knew Sanda. He was a violent alcoholic with multiple arrests for fighting and assaulting cops. Scotty's body, now pinned in the floor, blocked the door to the trailer and prevented his beat partner and backup from getting inside. As he tried to pull himself free, Scotty forced himself to look at Sanda's hands. "A man's hands can kill you, not his eyes," they'd told Scotty in the academy. Scotty's eyes locked on the bush axe in Sanda's left hand. Time stood still as Scotty saw the blade rise and watched the big man step toward him.

Afterward, Scotty didn't remember raising his weapon and firing. The official police report said he fired seven times, but he couldn't remember. He remembered the flash of the gun and the sensation of recoil as the slide on his Glock came back, the shell casings spinning up and right as the slide moved forward to chamber another round. When the man kept moving forward and took another step, Scotty remembered his training and the failure-to-stop drills he had practiced on the range so many times. He moved the gun up and fired twice at Sanda's face as he swung the bush axe. The man's head snapped back, and the blade missed Scotty by inches. Sanda fell dead and time slowly returned to normal. Scotty survived, but only because his training had taken over when he was trapped in that trailer. The homicide report determined that Sanda was twelve feet from Scotty when he fell through the floor. If he had hesitated, he would have been dead before the other officers could have helped him.

"She came to the precinct to show me her diploma. I was so proud of her."

"I know. I wish you could have truly understood the sense of accomplishment she felt when she walked across that stage to get her degree with her children watching her. Her youngest graduated the same week. College graduates three days and twenty-two years apart."

"It made the news."

"Yes. But that is what I mean, Scotty. Even in her darkest hours, she served the Lord by caring for and protecting her children. Her child served the Lord by secretly calling 911 and letting the operators hear what was happening inside that trailer."

"He was a brave little boy and so scared." Scotty recalled holding the boy close that night as they walked to the ambulance. He didn't think the boy would ever let go of him. He also feared the boy would never forgive him for killing his father.

"He is a police officer now, serving his community in Colorado. You didn't know that."

"Wow. He had a rough life at the start." Scotty took a breath and closed his eyes. "That makes me feel good to know that."

"He told the interview board when he was hired that a cop had saved his mother, his sisters, and himself one night, and because of that, he owed a debt to serve others."

For the first time in a long time, probably since he and Celina had lost Christine to cancer five years earlier, Scotty began to cry. He thought of the hundreds of kids he had seen in those same circumstances. He met them on domestic calls or at school presentations and would drive away saying a silent prayer that God would watch over them and give them a chance at a good life. He wept because he'd just learned his prayers were answered, and he wept for the others who probably had not survived their circumstances.

Some time passed as Scotty recovered. Somewhere in the midst of his tears, he felt Christ's arm around him. It was comforting and familiar. How many times throughout his life had he felt the comfort of Christ's arms in the midst of his despair and fear?

"Don't forget you and your backup officers."

Scotty looked up. "What do you mean?"

"They served the Lord by taking an oath to serve others, to put the safety of strangers above their own."

Scotty nodded. "They were good people." Scotty thought of the funeral for one of those young officers who had responded that night. He had been killed by a drunk driver as he sat at a red light in his patrol car.

Scotty was pulled from the memory of that funeral by Christ's words. "And you, Scotty. Don't forget yourself."

Scotty came back to the conversation, thankful to avoid thinking about that day. "What about me?"

"You chose to serve the Lord too, and you did. You were so scared as you approached that trailer that night. You knew the violence that man was capable of. You and two officers had arrested him weeks before because he nearly beat a man to death outside the bar next to the trailer park."

Scotty looked down. "I was scared a lot."

"Of course, you were. Fear is a part of life. Everyone feels afraid." Christ paused. "The Bible and preachers make much of temptation, Scotty. People are told of the temptations of sin and evil. I think people in church have been told to avoid temptation more than anything else. Temptation, Scotty, doesn't only apply to sins and things that are bad for you. Perhaps the biggest temptation in life is fear. It can be seductive, and once it gains a foothold, it becomes invasive. A moment of fear can change the course of a life. Our Father meant great things for all people, but sadly, most do not reach their potential because of fear. They may live sheltered lives or strike out at the people around them, but it is all due to fear. It is true that a life lived in fear is not a full life. You and many of your fellow officers, more than anything, pushed fear aside every day to fulfill your oaths and to protect others."

"It was my job."

"Lots of people have jobs, Scotty. Many people decide not to complete their jobs or do what they promised when the task is too hard or they are afraid. Others choose jobs that do not challenge them or require little, if any, effort. You moved forward and entered that trailer when you knew your life was in danger. You acted. Sanda had murder in his heart that night, Scotty. Tanya and her children would not have survived if you had hesitated entering that trailer." Christ paused. "You would not have survived if you had hesitated when he came at you."

Scotty knew the shooting had been ruled legally justified, but it had still taken him a long time to move on from those few horrific seconds. He'd spent many nights alone, reliving and analyzing that night, wondering if he could have found a way to survive without taking Sanda's life. Through all of the thoughts and hindsight, he had found no such solution.

"Your academy instructors served the Lord when they set their minds to teach you and your classmates how to protect yourselves and others."

"They saved my life. My training took over."

"Yes," Christ said. "And you served the Lord when you saved yourself, Tanya, and her children."

Christ's words struck a chord deep within Scotty Painter. It was a raw spot on his soul. In an instant, Scotty was flooded by intense pain and sorrow. Weeping seemed an inadequate response to the sensation. It was like the ripping of healed skin from an old and very deep wound. Scotty could barely breathe. After a long silence, Scotty spoke, his voice barely above a whisper.

"How could I serve the Lord by taking a life?" Scotty felt a lump in his throat, and his eyes began to water. His heart was heavy and his body felt weak. It was a question on his mind, in his heart, and on his lips that had remained unspoken for more than twenty years. He hadn't even been able to bring himself to ask his pastor in the confines of their private counseling sessions that went on for years after the shooting, even after he was cleared by the grand jury, and the media reports faded. Perhaps he was afraid of the answer or more afraid that no one would have an answer.

"Just because Charlton Heston said, 'Thou shalt not kill' doesn't mean that's what our Father said." Scotty watched as Jesus smiled. Scotty smiled too. He began to feel the tightness in his chest unwind.

"God's commandment was 'Thou shalt not commit murder.' As your Georgia law reads, murder requires a 'maligned heart.' I always found those words particularly accurate." Christ closed his eyes and took a deep breath in. He shook his head as he exhaled and stared at the water as he continued. "I've seen into the hearts of men and women before, during, and after they've murdered, Scotty. The act of murdering another was their sole purpose and goal. That desire drove both their thoughts and their actions. That night, Scotty, your actions were driven by a desire to protect seven innocent people."

"Seven?"

"Tanya and her children are four. You and your back-up officers are the other three." Christ looked back at Scotty. "He was planning to attack any officer who responded after he killed his family that night, and he would have been successful until someone stopped him. You had a short window of time to prevent that, Scotty, and you acted with the courage and conviction God gave you. You served the Lord with the skills He gave you and with the knowledge provided to you through the skills of others."

Both sat silently. Christ stared at the sea, and Scotty's mind drifted. He thought of the impact of that outcome. He envisioned three little caskets on display with the casket of their mother. He felt the immense sadness that would have enveloped the community surrounding the funerals of three officers. He also thought of the good done by Tanya and her three children, especially the one who was now out protecting others. Scotty took this all in.

"I understand now. I will always be sad that Sanda died, but I am glad we all survived."

"Me too, Scotty. Me too."

Chapter VI

For Every Journey Holds
Obstacles and We All Will Stumble

cotty must have dozed off into a deep sleep. It was at the same time restful and uneasy. What seemed like a dream also seemed so real. There was deep darkness, but he sensed movement. He felt like he should speak to the people he sensed around him, but he couldn't utter a sound. Then the pain returned, replacing any other sensation, ripping into him, relentless. The movement around him seemed to intensify as he tried to push through the pain as he had done all his life. That was how he had survived after being T-boned by a drunk driver nearly thirty years ago. He'd done the only thing that came naturally to him: fighting the pain and pushing back.

This was different. The more he pushed, the more the pain came in waves. He wanted to scream, but like any other nightmare, his screams were silent and ineffective. Bright lights seemed to penetrate the darkness that surrounded him. It felt as if he was being pinched on his arms. The pain and intensity of the lights increased until it seemed he could not bear another second. Then the nightmare was over, and he woke to feel the soft, warm sunlight on his face. Instantly, he was comforted to know he was back on the beach. Without a thought, he also knew Christ was still by his side.

"I've seen good people fall from grace." The words came from Scotty's lips effortlessly. A feeling so deep was brought to the surface. He seemed relieved to speak them, and his soul felt lighter.

"You have? Tell me."

"As a commander, my door was always open to my officers. So many of them came to me with personal problems. I was honored to listen and help when I could."

Christ nodded. "You never turned them away. That meant a lot to them."

"I suppose, but sometimes I could do nothing for them. Their indiscretions cost them their careers. Some recovered; some did not." Scotty paused and looked at Christ. "Did I do enough for them?"

Christ stood and reached down to Scotty. "Let's take a walk. You'll feel better." Scotty took the hand extended to him and stood. He thought to himself that the pain he'd felt must have been just a very bad dream. He was pain-free and felt great. He welcomed a walk on the soft, warm sand.

They walked for a while in silence, watching the water roll onto the beach. It seemed as endless as time itself, always rolling, covering every part of every beach everywhere. Scotty thought how there was something comforting in that. The sea was like God's love. It never stopped, and it was always there for you. If you strayed from it, you only needed to point yourself towards Him and return to the comfort of the certainty that His love and grace would always be there. Even when you were miles from the beach, the water always rolled onto the sand.

"Which of their personal problems were the hardest for you to hear, Scotty?"

"When they became addicted to alcohol or prescription drugs—that was hard. But the toughest times for me was when their indiscretions led to them break the law. DUI charges, domestic violence arrests, it was hard to see that. It was even harder to know that their careers were over. They sacrificed so much to get to that point."

Christ thought about Scotty's words and nodded. "You helped them with your compassion, Scotty. You also gave many of them guidance that helped them get back on their feet later in life."

"I hope so. Each of those talks took a lot out of me. I listened even when I didn't agree and couldn't condone their actions. Many times, I had no answers for them."

"Sometimes people came to you seeking only to un-burden themselves, not for answers."

Scotty pondered this thought. "It's understandable, you know. They changed because of the things they saw and the job they had to do. Putting bodies in bags, seeing the carnage of DUI drivers, hearing the last breaths of people when they got there a second too late to save them. It's a hard life."

Christ just listened. He did as Scotty had done all those times in his office. He allowed Scotty to pass his burdens onto him.

"The hardest part is doing all of those things—knowing that people expected them to respond to calls for help—while hearing the criticisms and feeling the hate when they emerged from their patrol cars at the scene. That proved too much for so many good people, and they fell. Some fell hard."

"Indeed they fell, Scotty. But why do you believe they fell from grace?"

Scotty thought of the pain on their faces, the sorrow as they handed in their badges and left the department for the last time. Many resigned to avoid the inevitable—termination. They chose to tender their resignations to him. While that made him proud to be trusted, it was a tremendous burden. He struggled with how to explain the point that Christ seemed to be missing.

"They lost everything: their careers, their pride, the respect of their peers, and many times, their families as well."

"Go on."

The conversation that had seemed to be effortless took a new turn. He found himself working to find the right words to make his point and convince Christ. "Their actions caused some of them to be vilified in the media and in their communities. A few were forced to move from the city or the state to have a chance at a normal life."

"Is there more, Scotty?"

Scotty was puzzled. Why was Christ pressuring him? He thought about all of the officers who had come to him in his thirty years wearing the badge.

"Some went to prison for their actions. We even had an officer from a neighboring jurisdiction who became addicted to pornography and unknowingly downloaded a video of sixteen-year-old runaways who had been forced into the porn industry. He was labeled a pedophile, went to federal prison for twenty-two years, and will have to report as a sex offender for the rest of his life if he survives in prison."

Christ looked on and said nothing. Scotty felt compelled to go further.

"I read stories about people in our community who were alcoholics who beat their children. One even killed his wife." He had moved on from personal examples to any example he could think of to show Christ that he was right.

Scotty looked at Christ, who said nothing. Scotty stood nearly exhausted. He had described these horrible things done by good people who had ruined their lives and the lives of others. He was mentally spent and could not think of another thing to say.

As Scotty stood silent, Christ looked into his eyes.

"You said you saw good people fall from grace. Grace is the unconditional love of God, Scotty. They may have done horrible things. They may have destroyed the lives they built, their reputations, their careers, and the trust placed in them by others. They may have abandoned their values and violated their oaths, disappointed their families and friends, and become the target of intense hatred and apathy." Christ put both his hands on Scotty's shoulders. After a moment, he continued. "But they could never destroy the unconditional love of our Father, Scotty. No one has the power to take that away."

Scotty sat down on the sand. He stared at the water. He recalled all of the times he'd become angry at the people he'd described for what they did and their weakness in failing to remain true and loyal to their friends, their families, and themselves. He was now filled with both clarity and regret. Had he judged them? Had he failed them when they came to him seeking understanding? He thought hard about his facial expressions and body language in those conversations. So little communication takes place in the form of words. Did his body send a message of understanding or condemnation? Did he judge them because he believed they fell from grace?

"They knew your heart, Scotty."

"I don't understand."

"They didn't expect you to have answers, Scotty. Not you, the counselors, the pastors, or priests. You could only offer guidance, but the answers were always inside of them if they only looked. Some eventually realized and understood. Others struggled and denied the truth their whole lives."

"If I understood, perhaps I could have done more to help them. Maybe I would have been motivated to take that extra step." Scotty dropped his head and stared at the sand.

"The souls of men and women need little guidance from others, Scotty. Children want to be good people, and adults want to be better people. It is when they turn from what they know is right and good that they find themselves wandering and lost for answers."

Scotty was comforted by these words. "So there is hope for all of them?"

"Always, Scotty. You have heard these words before. 'I shall not forsake you, neither shall I let go of your hand.'"

Scotty remembered. He also remembered the story of the shepherd who lost one sheep of a flock of one hundred. He endured hardships to find his lost sheep and rejoiced when he returned the sheep to the flock. As he recalled the story, Christ spoke.

"As Matthew told, not only the shepherd rejoiced but all of his friends as well. And God rejoiced too, Scotty. What hardships would you endure, what lengths would you go to if Celina needed your help?"

"Anything. I would cross the desert on my hands and knees and risk my life a thousand times over."

"So it is with the Father. There is no divide wide enough, no distance sufficient to separate God from the love for His children. Though these people you remember may have fallen hard, in the eyes of God, they have only stumbled. The grace of God remains. They need only have hope and faith in that love to receive the blessings of His grace."

Scotty thought about these words. They provided so much hope. He wondered why this message was not in the forefront of all Christian teachings. How many more would turn back toward God if they only understood?

"Life presents so many challenges, hardships, and opportunities, Scotty. People can become shining examples of God's love or destroy all that is around them. That is why it is so important for parents to love their children and help them grow. That is why it is important for all people to find ways to help, support, and protect each other. While the wicked cannot escape the grace of

God, they live sad and tortured lives when they deny themselves access to it."

Scotty nodded his head. He understood and had seen many times the senseless examples of the sad and tortured lives Christ described. "There's something else. I let a few people down even after they were gone."

"What do you mean, 'after they were gone'?"

"I remember attending a funeral for a deputy who took his own life. He was retired at the time, but he was still a law enforcement officer. I remember walking into the church, afraid I would be the only one there. The church was a few blocks from police headquarters, so I didn't see a lot of cars outside. As I walked in, I saw a bunch of people; I mean the chapel was full! That's when I got mad."

"Why were you mad?"

"I thought about all of the people there and how any of them, including me, would have picked up the telephone in the middle of night to have helped him, to have talked to him. That's when I got mad. Mad that he didn't call any of us, mad that he made us attend a funeral, and mad that we had no answers as to why he took his own life."

Christ nodded. "There were a lot of mixed emotions in that church that day, Scotty. You were not the only one."

"I'm sure of that, because then my anger turned to guilt. How could I be anything other than sad at his passing?"

"Our hearts are capable of feeling many things at the same time, Scotty. You were working through a lot of very difficult emotions. That is a hard thing to do, but through that process, we learn about ourselves and what is most important to us."

The words began in the back of Scotty's throat and slowly passed his lips. They were nearly inaudible. "He was such a tortured soul. Will God ever forgive him for taking his own life?"

Christ stopped walking and closed his eyes. For the first time, Scotty thought he seemed to be in pain. After a few moments, he opened his eyes and spoke. "Sometimes, the life a person lives is filled with burdens too heavy to bear. The burdens that may make one person stronger are enough to crush another. God knew his heart at the moment he passed, and I felt his desperation. He took his own life to escape the pain he felt, Scotty. It had enveloped his life. It is sad and unthinkable, but he saw no other way to escape that pain. But in the eyes of God, his soul is worthy of salvation and God's grace will be there for him as it was throughout his life."

A silence passed between them. Scotty felt a need to give Christ time to recover. The words he spoke so easily clearly worked an injury to his heart. Scotty saw it on his face and in his eyes.

"You said it hurts to see people make bad choices and to hurt each other."

"Indeed, Scotty. It is a pain that is hard to describe and sometimes even harder to escape."

"I understand now why you and our Father do not intervene and keep people from doing terrible things, but why don't you keep them from hurting themselves? Isn't that harder to watch, seeing them throw away everything they will ever have?"

Christ was again silent for a few moments. "Of all the things the Father stands by and allows when His children make bad decisions, suicide is perhaps the most painful."

"Why?"

"When one of His children takes his own life, they destroy a future filled with possibilities and promise. Each life is sacred, Scotty, and each life is worth living. Sometimes a suicide leaves Him struggling for answers just like the family of the person who dies."

"But you can see into the person's heart and understand why they did it."

"Understanding and wishing for a different future are two different things, Scotty. It's like the death of a child from a disease or at the hands of a person. The sadness is overwhelming and unavoidable."

Scotty thought about that for a moment. He could recall very few single suicides that were telegraphed in advance. The person was nearly always found by a relative or friend after the fact. As a hostage negotiator, he learned that some people cannot be dissuaded from taking their own lives even if they call 911 before they commit the act. He spoke now with a new purpose: to comfort Christ in his sadness, regretting that he raised the subject but knowing that Christ wanted him to ask.

"I know how painful it is for the people left behind. I can only imagine how hard it is to know it is about to happen and be unable to stop it."

"I have seen a suicide bring our Father to tears, Scotty."

The image of God crying had never entered into Scotty's mind before this. He had seen paintings and drawings and read descriptions of God. In all of them, He was mostly happy and sometimes angry. The wrath of God was always discussed, sometimes frequently between Scotty and his grandmother when he was a particularly curious young boy. He wondered why no one ever envisioned or described God's sadness.

Christ's last words had long faded from Scotty's ears. His face returned to the flush look of contentment and happiness. Scotty was thankful.

"You have more questions, Scotty. Don't be afraid to continue."

Scotty nodded. He thought about the struggles of his friend who committed suicide and others he feared would do the same but turned their lives around.

"Why are some people able to overcome hardship better than others? Why are some so strong in the face of temptation when others seem to fail so easily?"

"Why can some people run faster, climb higher, and endure more pain? Life itself takes many forms, Scotty. For many, the struggle of life is making it to work in rush-hour traffic or even looking for a job. For others, like the soldier, it may be surviving to see another sunrise. Some think those who dig deepest in time of struggle are extraordinary people, but that's not true. Every person has the ability to surpass the expectations of those around them and themselves. The young person who cries himself to sleep the first night at Parris Island may become the one person who saves the lives of hundreds of other Marines. It's part of the choices we discussed."

"Some people are more focused than others."

"Yes and some have more skills, but all people are capable of achieving great things. They need only awaken their inner drive and will."

"How? Why are some seemingly unable to do it?"

"Some do it through the help of others like their parents, their teachers, their pastors, or a person they meet who motivates them. Others do it through faith."

Scotty nodded. He felt like he was starting to understand and see a bigger picture. It was like he gained a broader, more informed, cogent view of the world and the people in his life.

"Faith is not just faith in God, Scotty. People must have faith in themselves and why they are on Earth living their lives. That is why strength is so important. Faith is a partnership between God and man." Christ paused. "A team like that can never be defeated." Christ winked at Scotty, who smiled.

Scotty seemed refreshed and alive, unburdened. He took a deep, long breath in and exhaled slowly. The air seemed to lift him. He felt Christ's arm on his shoulder and opened his eyes.

"Come, Scotty. Let's keep walking. We have so much more to talk about."

They walked silently down the beach toward the mountains in the distance. Scotty enjoyed their discussions but was thankful for the silence. He had a lot to think about. For the first time in his life, he felt that he had the time to do so. No phone, no obligations, no decisions waiting for him. He turned and headed down the beach, the smell of the salt air seeming to carry him across the sand as the hand of Christ supported him. Scotty knew it was not the first time and somehow was certain it would not be the last.

Chapter VII

Deeds Done in Haste
and Work Left Unfinished

W hen I was a commander, I sent men and women into deadly confrontations. I knew these people, their spouses, and their children. In some cases, I knew their parents. How can we make choices and decisions in haste without knowing the outcome?"

Christ listened and closed his eyes. "You're thinking of more than your time with the police department, aren't you, Scotty?"

Scotty was sitting against a large rock at the edge of the sand. The beautiful beach seemed to yield to the soft, green grass, then extend toward the mountains. Scotty's mind recalled the SWAT callout, the decision to breach the door, the lives of hostages hanging in the balance of his decision. He also recalled the funerals, one ending with a flyover and a bugler playing "Taps."

"Of course. I've made many decisions outside the police department as a father, a husband, a friend, and a son. How can we live with the consequences when we did not have a clear decision and all the information we needed before us?"

"God created you in His image, Scotty. Do you know what that means?"

"I always thought that meant God was just as goofy looking as I am," Scotty said as he chuckled. Christ laughed too.

"Image is more than physical appearance, Scotty. People have tremendous power and ability within them. They can show boundless compassion, love unconditionally, and think about the wonders of the world. They can ponder the future, consider their path in life, and change the paths of others. You've seen people, brilliant people, transform the lives of others through their actions. They invent marvelous things that end suffering and give hope to millions."

Scotty thought about the stories of people who eradicated diseases and others who found the strength to sacrifice for others. He thought about the officers he knew who spent their off-time working with troubled youth.

"Yes," Christ said, seeming to see the images in Scotty's mind. "But there's so much more than that."

"Think of the people who made decisions that made history. Churchill, Lincoln, Reagan, Moses, and Peter."

"And you," Scotty said. "You made a decision. You walked among us and had the power to raise the dead. You could have prevented your crucifixion."

"Yes, Scotty. And just like me, they made a decision to trust in the Lord. I could not foresee all the good and bad that came after my death. The birth of the church, the fall of the Roman Empire, the Inquisition, the rise of Hitler."

"I thought you always knew what man would do."

"I always know, Scotty, what man *can* do. Free choice makes the future unpredictable." Scotty let Christ's words sink in.

"How was I equipped to make those decisions? What about all the times Celina came to me, not knowing which way to turn with her life, her studies, and her career? I felt so inadequate knowing her decisions would affect the rest of her life!"

"You were made in the image of a loving Father, Scotty. You were given the gifts of rational thought, kindness, and empathy. You had the capacity to love and have faith. These are the tools needed to make those decisions, Scotty."

Scotty pondered Christ's answer. "And when that raid went wrong, when we lost our officer . . . " Scotty's words trailed off. His throat was tight. "Did I let Him down?" The words ran from him like blood from a wound.

Christ moved toward Scotty. "Every event in your life led you to that moment, Scotty. Every decision, every effort you took to study and learn what to do in that instance, guided your decision. But that's not all, Scotty. Your heart also guided you. Yes, you knew the risks, and so did those brave men and women who followed your orders. Their lives took a path that led them to that moment as well. Hours of training and preparation."

"Was I wrong?"

The question lingered between them for what seemed like an eternity. Finally, Christ spoke softly.

"Sometimes life presents circumstances that can only end in disappointment and sorrow. A child dies at birth. A good Samaritan helping a drowning victim in a flood is swept away."

Christ picked up his head and looked directly at Scotty. The silence between them grew nearly uncomfortable.

"Sometimes a good and faithful wife and mother succumbs to a deadly disease, and her loving husband must decide to let her go."

The words struck Scotty quickly like a flash of light. In a moment, he was back in Christine's hospital room, staring at the paper on the clipboard. He read the words like he was seeing them for the first time: "Allow natural death." He watched as his hand signed the line above the word "Husband" that had been written in by the nurse.

Scotty felt drained. "There was no good choice to make. She was in pain and never would have regained consciousness." Scotty slumped over, nearly falling onto the ground.

"Yes, Scotty. But you used the gifts God gave you to make the horrible choice to let her go."

"It's what she wanted. She was so afraid of the pain, and they could do nothing to take it away anymore."

"I know, Scotty, but she is free of that pain now. You see, you used the skills you were given to make a choice. Just like that day at the hostage scene, and when Celina nearly dropped out of college. God does not judge the decisions you make when you have used the skills and emotions he gave you."

"Celina. She's still so young. I hope and pray each day that she has the skills necessary to get her through her life."

"She's a bright woman with a strong sense of right and wrong."

"You've got that right! She's made mistakes, but she never did some of the dumb things I did growing up."

Christ smiled. Scotty smiled too.

"I've always been there to help and protect her even when she didn't realize the dangers."

Scotty thought about his daughter. When Celina was a little girl, she was always staring in wonder at the smallest things: a bicycle on the street, a puppy, or a crack in the sidewalk. Christine always told her to pay attention as they approached the street, but Scotty was fascinated by the way she could focus on the smallest details of the ordinary things around her. So, rather than make her think she was not allowed to wonder at the world around her, she and Scotty worked out a signal when they approached the street corner. If they were safe to cross, he would squeeze her hand twice, real quickly. At that signal, Celina would pick her head up and pay attention to the traffic. It was their agreement. It was always between them.

When he walked her to the altar on her wedding day, he held her hand. It was a spontaneous gesture at the back of the church. Tradition said he should present his arm, and she would grab it at the elbow.

"Let's start our own tradition," Celina said. "What's the pastor going to do? Refuse to marry us?"

They both laughed and Scotty dropped his arm. Celina took his left hand in her right and they walked down the aisle. As they approached the altar, Scotty stopped. He looked at his beautiful daughter and quickly squeezed her hand twice. He wasn't sure which one of them was more in danger of losing it, but somehow they kept it together.

"How can I know that I've taught her everything I can? I mean, she's still so young."

"Just like you, she started with a good foundation. You and Christine guided her as she grew, and so did lots of others, but remember, Scotty, she too was created in God's image."

Scotty thought about part of what Christ said to him. He recalled the many times she came to the precinct and met so many "aunts and uncles" in uniform. All the picnics, fundraisers, and Fraternal Order of Police events and conferences they attended seemed to provide Celina with an endless sea of good people who wanted her to succeed. When she was in a wreck her senior year of college, she called Scotty, and, of course, he arrived as quickly as he could. He was a major at the time. When he arrived, there were about ten uniform patrol cars on the scene checking on her. The paramedics had loaded her into the ambulance, but she refused to leave the scene until her daddy got there. Celina was part of a family. She was a good woman because of everyone she knew, and she had learned something from each of them.

"She loved going to see you at work, didn't she?"

"Yes. My favorite thing was to see the six-foot-five motor officer kneel down to hug her, or the female lieutenant with her hair pulled back into a tight bun warm up when Celina came into the room. She spent a lot of time sitting on people's laps. They were such good folks."

Scotty stopped for a moment. He had just mentioned the people he worked with in the past tense. They "were" good folks. He had been a sharp detective during his time in homicide and recognized the words as soon as they left his lips. Christ noticed it too and broke the silence that had started between them.

"Let's turn this way."

They turned up a lush green field toward a mountain. Scotty was a hunter, and he knew that walking up such a mountain would require a lot of effort. However, his feet seemed light and his breathing never became labored. Each step brought them closer to the top of the mountain. The rich green grass was interrupted a few hundred yards away by a field of wildflowers that reminded him of his first home with Christine. She had bought wildflower seeds the weekend they got engaged and spread them in a field behind their first house four years later.

"We probably won't live here forever, but these flowers will," she said. "Wildflowers keep on blooming even if no one takes care of them."

Scotty thought, in that moment so many years ago, how beautiful she was. He recalled the moment like it was only a moment ago. He looked at the field of wildflowers and the pink, yellow, and purple petals. *Someone takes care of them,* he thought. *We just don't always see His hands.*

Suddenly the enjoyable walk was interrupted. Scotty felt like someone had pulled the breath out of his lungs, and his gut was on fire. He fell to his knees. His eyes were open, but all he could see was white from the pain. He tried to breathe through the pain as he had done before, but he could not get any air. In that instant, Scotty started to panic.

The transition from the tranquil and effortless walk up the mountain to the feeling of panic reminded him of so many hot calls he'd received on the radio as a patrol officer. How many times had a beautiful spring day been interrupted by a call of a shooting, a robbery, or an officer needing help? If he was honest, that is what he hated about the job. The adrenaline high he'd felt as a twenty-two-year-old cop had long worn off. Once he learned of the carnage that likely awaited his arrival, he was less excited about the call and more focused on praying for a safe response and outcome. Scotty always wondered if the public knew just how much praying takes place in police cars—more in the front seat than in the back.

Unlike the previous episodes of pain, Scotty soon accepted that this one would not pass so easily. Scotty rolled onto his side and tried to breathe.

"Breathe out first, Scotty," Christ said. Scotty had nearly forgotten that he was not alone. That's how it is with true pain. It robs you of your senses and the only two things you know are the pain and the hope of relief.

Scotty forced himself to push just a bit of air out of his lungs. He was then able to take a deep breath and his vision began to clear. He was still on the ground.

"That's it. Take your time. A few more breaths and you'll feel much better."

On the fourth or fifth breath, Scotty began to return to the beauty and peacefulness of his surroundings. His body was soaked with sweat. He sat up and felt the need to apologize.

"Sorry. I couldn't help it."

"It's OK. There's no rush."

"I don't know what that was, but I don't want anymore!" Scotty quipped, trying to cheer himself up.

Christ sat silently on a rock. He watched while Scotty regained his composure and stood.

"What do you think? Ready to keep going?"

"Of course, I was just waiting for you to catch your breath!" It was an old and favorite joke he'd used many times while hunting in Montana with guides who seemed more mountain goat than mountain man.

Christ smiled. "I've always loved your sense of humor, Scotty. It helped you through many tough times in your life. It will help you now. Don't give up on it."

The thought seemed strange to Scotty. Christ referred to two separate time frames: his life and now. Perhaps he was being too analytical, but he couldn't turn it off. He was a cop through and through. He decided to put off that thought as they reached the peak. *How long have we been climbing?* he thought.

As they stepped onto the peak of the tall mountain, Scotty was nearly blinded again. This time it was not a blinding pain or bright sunlight. Scotty was blinded by the beauty before him. Scotty thought of the words from Ecclesiastes: *He has made everything beautiful in its time.* It was beautiful, from the ocean in front of him to the other mountains behind him and the deep blue lakes in the valley. He felt small even though he seemed to be standing at the top of the world.

Chapter VIII

What Have I Done
with the Gifts God Gave Me?

I've read so many books and heard so many sermons by spiritual leaders claiming that man cannot understand the beauty of Heaven. Why do they say that?" Christ asked.

Scotty had no idea how long they had stood silently before Christ spoke. The feeling of wonder at the beauty before him was the closest thing he ever felt to intoxication without touching a drop of alcohol. He realized that this was the first question Christ asked him that was not in furtherance of their conversation. Did he really not know? Was he really asking Scotty to explain something to him?

"Not sure. I suspect it's because some people need to believe that Heaven is more beautiful and peaceful than they could possibly imagine or comprehend." Scotty paused and thought for a moment. "Maybe it's easier to believe in something that is incapable of description."

Christ pondered his answer. "What do you believe?"

Scotty thought for a moment but was surprised when the words began to form in his throat.

"Well, I think people misinterpret the words 'for the Lord has prepared a home for you.' I do not imagine a home in the sense of four sturdy walls. Some people might, however, if they never had such a home. If our bodies stay on Earth, and only our souls rise, what would we do with a physical house?"

Christ looked on as Scotty continued.

"I think Heaven is a place where there is no pain. I don't mean just physical pain but any type of pain. Pain in the form of worry, discomfort, insecurity; fear is probably the first thing that will vanish when we arrive. Maybe it is different things to different people. For the person who was not able to walk, maybe their heaven is being able to run free. For the person who knew only hunger, perhaps they will have no fear of living without a meal. I know I never believed in the check-in desk."

"The check-in desk? What do you mean? That's a new one!" Christ began to laugh. It was the first time Scotty had heard him really laugh spontaneously. His smile warmed the heart, but Christ's laugh filled every inch of Scotty's soul.

Scotty went on, encouraged by Christ's reaction. He felt like he was back in the squad room cutting up with his shift. He could feel his body lighten up as he continued.

"You know! The theory that Saint Peter is waiting at the pearly gates to check you into Heaven. I always thought that was weird and quite impractical—I mean look at how many people die each day. It would take forever. It took me twenty minutes to check into Caesar's Palace in Las Vegas once. Could you just imagine how long people would be standing in line at the pearly gates? I mean, Peter would need two million desk agents just to keep up! Remember, people had waited a long time to get there. They would not want to stand in line for too long, but who's going to complain? What are they going to do, ask to see the manager?"

Scotty had cracked himself up. He started laughing for the first time in a long time, really laughing. He looked over and Christ was laughing too! The two laughed until tears rolled down their faces like two childhood friends sharing an old joke recalled from years past.

"I never thought about that, but you have a point. People have used the pearly gates for much amusement. They have been the setting for countless jokes over the years. Why do you think that is?"

"I guess, like anything else, people joke about things that make them wonder or make them feel insecure. I mean, that thought is pretty intimidating. What if you make it through your life and get to the pearly gates only to find out that you have no reservation, so to speak? What if you've done something in your life that prevented you from entering? I guess some people need that pressure to keep them from temptation."

"That's a good theory. I guess that's as good as any." Christ's laughter turned back into a warm smile. "What about you? Do you believe in a gatekeeper?"

"Well," Scotty cleared his throat and wiped away the last tears from his eyes, "like anything else, I believe we are not judged by the single episodes in our lives, good or bad. I always felt that life is full of opportunities and each of us brings something to the table. It's like a barn raising. Some people are great at designing the barn and others at hammering nails. If you seek every opportunity to use the skills God gave you by looking for those barn raisings, you will not be banished from Heaven because you didn't plane the boards as long as you used your hammering skills. I think God even forgives you if you turn the air blue when you hit your thumb! After all, if you hammer enough nails, you'll curse at some point."

Christ smiled again. "Well said, Scotty. I've certainly seen my share of blue air around people doing good deeds."

Scotty's face drew down. He was fixated on a thought. His eyes slowly began to fill with tears and a sense of uncertainty filled him. It was like the feeling you get in your hands and feet as you approach the edge of a tall building. Scotty looked at Christ as he spoke.

"What about me and my life? Have I hammered enough nails? Have I used the skills God gave me to help others? Did I seek out enough opportunities to improve people's lives?" His head sank lower. "Did I squander my gifts?"

Christ watched as tears began to run down Scotty's face.

"Of all the human emotions—fear, anxiety, hate—I wish I could do away with insecurity." Christ moved to Scotty and hugged him. It was a hug filled with the passion of a father for a child, knowing no bounds and feeling at once intensely powerful and comforting. Scotty wept as time stood still. Just a man and his savior together, exactly as God intended.

Scotty caught his breath and the men separated, but only by a few feet. Scotty sat down. He felt drained but also unburdened.

"I don't know what came over me. It's a fear I've had my whole life. What if I was too busy doing things that didn't really matter?"

"God gave you a life so that you could live it. Like most people, you helped when you saw a need, but you went above that. Like the soldier, the firefighter, and other public servants, you chose to live your professional life in service to others."

"But that was my job."

"It was your calling, Scotty. You recognized you had skills. Skills to speak with people, learn about them, lead them, and don't forget your bravery."

"I was never brave, really."

"Bravery is doing your job or putting yourself at risk to help others when your fear pleads with you to go no further."

"If that's the definition, I guess I was the bravest of them all. I've been so scared I thought my knees were going to bend backwards!" Scotty started to smile. Christ smiled too.

"There's no ledger, Scotty. Some people go through their entire lives without using the skills they were given. Others spend their days seeking opportunities to do so. You didn't waste your gifts, Scotty. Far from it."

The words were comforting to Scotty and he focused on them. Like so many words Christ spoke, he found they struck deep in his soul.

"Don't forget the efforts you took to provide for the future of others. Celina will live a fuller life because of all the days and nights you spent with her. From efforts to help her with her homework to her questions about her career, you were there and used your gifts to guide her."

Scotty settled back and lay against the warm rock. The sun felt great on his body, especially his face. How many times had he asked those questions silently without an answer? How many times had he wondered if his life was on a good track? How many times had he secretly hoped that Saint Peter would not be standing at the pearly gates with a ledger? As these thoughts passed through his mind, he drifted off. It was a peaceful sleep.

Chapter IX
Decisions at the Crossroads

The sun on Scotty's face consumed his dreams. In a span of seconds, he was fishing with his dad, then walking across the campus with Celina after she received her college diploma. It was the type of dreaming that creates pleasant memories the next day—nothing specific, just a thought that a dream took place. Like many other dreams, the common thread was undeniable: being safe and happy.

The sunlight turned to a low glare in the windshield of his unmarked car. It was summer and the sun set late. He left the office late that day feeling good about his accomplishments. The command staff had finally finished the interviews for the sergeant and lieutenant candidates. As deputy chief, he was in charge of the promotion boards. While sometimes it felt like herding cats, juggling schedules to make it happen, he recognized the importance of the exercise. These were the next line of leaders.

He was in no hurry to get home. Since Christine passed, he spent most of his evenings and nights working out, reading, or writing his book on police procedure. Tonight was an off night for exercise. It was always that way with Wednesdays. Somehow, a rest in the middle of the week put more intensity into the rest of his workouts. As he drove down Clabash Avenue and toward the interstate, he was relaxed and looking forward to a quiet evening.

Scotty's mind began to wander ahead to the rest of his evening. He would drive the thirty minutes home, park in the driveway, and go into the house. It was quiet now. After Christine passed and Celina moved out, the house seemed to be missing its heart. Over the years they'd had dogs in the house, either family pets or Scotty's K9 partners, so he was never really alone in the house. Now, that was the norm, and the hardwoods echoed the silence of loneliness each evening when Scotty came in and walked to his bedroom.

On the days when he worked out, Scotty got a fair amount of contact with *regular people*. He chuckled as he thought about that term. One of his academy instructors told the class the first day that after the academy, none of them would ever be normal again. He explained that in order to survive, cops had to learn to think differently than the average person on the street. They learned to be more observant, more curious, and sadly, more suspicious than the citizens around them.

"My job is to teach you to keep your heads up and your eyes moving, and how to avoid getting your tails shot off!"

Scotty smiled. He could not believe that he remembered that line from so many years ago. While he swore that would never happen to him, the old instructor was right. A person can only read so many statements of convicted cop-killers, watch so many videos of cops being murdered simply because they wore the badge, and attend so many funerals listening to bagpipes and watching police helicopters flyover before the reality sets in. If cops want to stay alive and protect the public, they need to develop the skills to observe, inquire, and be on alert. Like every habit, however, there is a downside; they never look at the world the same way again. Scotty had picked up these skills quickly and was thankful that he did. As a field training officer, he had to "wash out" a few recruits who did not understand these basic truths. That was tough on Scotty, but he knew the price of letting them pass through. He was reminded of the cost with every cop funeral he attended.

While Scotty agreed with the advice of the crusty old academy instructor, he disagreed completely with the statement he made next on that first day so many years ago.

"After a while, if you make it through the academy and stay alive long enough, you'll reach a time in your career where your only friends are other cops, your spouse gave up long ago trying to understand you, and the best you can hope is that your dog still loves you."

It was those words that echoed with Scotty as he drove. The first prediction had nearly come to fruition: most of his friends were cops. He worked hard to maintain relationships outside the office through his rowing club, the shooting competitions he attended, and the people he'd met as Celina grew up. The second prediction never made sense to him. Christine was always so willing to listen and always knew when that was all Scotty needed. She once told him that she wanted to know about his work even though she knew she might learn things that frightened her. The instructor's last prediction was true throughout Scotty's life.

In common terms, Scotty was a dog person. He and Christine got a beautiful lab puppy, Mr. Biscuit, on their first anniversary. It was their "fur child" that prepared them, somewhat, for Celina's arrival. As they both grew, Celina and Mr. Biscuit became the best of friends. Scotty's K9 partner, Fritz, joined the mix without a hitch. There was something about having a dog in the house. That old academy instructor was right about that: pups always seemed to know what you needed. Scotty knew he was fortunate that his dogs were not his only support.

As he thought about how lucky he was throughout his career to have the support of friends and family, his mind snapped back to the reality of the empty home that awaited him. That's when Celina's words came into the forefront of his mind.

"It's OK to ask a woman to dinner, Dad. You're a good catch."

Those words made him so proud of her. She never lectured him about dating or moving on with his life romantically. She seemed to gently nudge him in that direction when the time seemed right. This last time, she was having coffee with him, and he had just described Rachel, a woman he met at the last rowing club event. Rachel was a writer. She freelanced for magazines and had done some ghostwriting early in her career, although most people knew her from the three crime novels she had penned. She was very intelligent and driven. For the first time in many years, Scotty could not deny the feeling of mutual attraction. Celina saw it on his face when he mentioned her.

"It's been a long time since I asked a woman out on a date, Celina."

"I know, but you deserve to be happy, Dad. Take a chance. You only regret the ones you don't take. Do you remember who told me that?"

"OK. Not fair using your old man's words against him!"

They finished their coffee with small talk, but they both knew something had changed. A barrier had been broken. Perhaps it was a mutual recognition that the time was right for Scotty to explore the next chapter in his life.

"That's it." He said out loud. "I'll call her as soon as I get home." The words came easier than he imagined and Scotty smiled. Tomorrow would be a brighter day, and he had so much to look forward to in his life. He turned right onto the entrance ramp and for the first time in years, he was eager to get home.

As Scotty accelerated to highway speeds, he saw blue lights in the distance. It was not uncommon, as the patrol units ran a lot of laser in this area. *Someone in a hurry to get home,* he thought. He had heard the traffic unit go out on the radio with the traffic stop as he turned onto the entrance ramp to the interstate. Like every officer, he listened to the tone and speed of the cop's voice, as well as the words. It all sounded like a typical traffic stop, but Scotty started to get that feeling. He had learned not to ignore it and took his foot off the accelerator. As he approached the patrol unit on the right shoulder, he saw the horror that keeps officers awake at night.

Scotty crested a small hill and saw the patrol unit behind a sedan. The car was about five years old but had seen better days. Scotty slowed a bit and looked in his mirrors to confirm the right lane was clear in case he had to move over. Something was bothering him as he approached, but he couldn't put his finger on it. It all seemed normal until he got even with the patrol car. That's when he saw the uniformed officer on the ground with a massive suspect behind him. The suspect's left arm was choking the officer, and his right hand was trying to remove his service weapon from the security holster. In one smooth move, Scotty picked up the radio microphone, moved over one lane, braked hard, and spoke to Radio.

"Cruiser Two, emergency. 90 West just past Clabash. Officer needs help!" Years of experience had taught him to be calm, and his words were even and deliberate.

"Roger, Cruiser Two. Any unit in the area of 90 West past Clabash, Cruiser Two requesting assistance for a Signal 63. Be advised Unit 3035 is on a traffic stop in that area."

As Scotty pulled onto the right shoulder, he heard the radio begin to come alive. Units from three jurisdictions were heading his way. *The highway is clear*, Scotty thought. *They'll be here quickly, and it could not be soon enough.*

As Scotty exited his car, he saw the suspect's posture change. His body went lower, and Scotty knew what that meant: the officer was unconscious. Scotty ran around the suspect's car with his Glock in his right hand. He quickly swept the suspect's car and found it empty. He also saw the broken steering column. *Stolen*, he thought. He tried to process who this guy was. It made a difference. Could he be talked down, or was he out to kill a cop that day?

As Scotty came around the right rear of the suspect's car, he was prepared to take a position and shoot if the suspect was still choking the officer. His mind prepared for the battle, and he forced himself to breathe in and out in big, full breaths. He only hoped that the suspect had not been able to defeat the security of the officer's holster. As he rounded the right rear of the suspect's vehicle, he saw that he was too late.

The first round hit Scotty between his vest and his belt. The second and third hit his body armor, and the last clipped his left collarbone. Although the force of the rounds pushed him back, Scotty started firing. He sensed the impact but felt no pain.

Scotty hit the suspect five times in less than a second. He could see the suspect's shirt puffing out as the shots entered his body, but the bullets seemed to have no effect. Time stood still as the men fired at each other less than fifteen feet apart.

Scotty saw the shell casings from his .45 spinning slowly up and to the right. He watched the slide on his weapon come back and move forward as another round peeled from the magazine into the chamber. He was acutely aware of the smell of gunpowder, but he could not hear any gunshots. Both his gun and the suspect's weapon seemed to be silent or making slight popping noises. Scotty knew he was developing tunnel vision, and that could be deadly. "Breathe," he told himself as he took in another breath.

The suspect was massive. Scotty's mind was formulating a description as he focused the front sight for the next shot. The man was easily six foot five and three hundred pounds. He still held the officer in the crook of his left arm like a ragdoll. Scotty knew he had to put the suspect down, or at least keep his fire directed at Scotty. The officer on the ground had no chance to fight if the suspect turned the gun toward him, and if he continued choking him, the officer could die or suffer permanent brain damage.

Scotty continued to fire, aiming at the suspect's torso which was the largest target available to him. He had to make certain that he did not hit the unconscious officer. His mind contemplated a head shot, but that was too risky. He would be shooting toward traffic and might hit a passerby. Scotty focused his mind on the center of the suspect's chest as he fell against the right rear corner of the suspect's vehicle.

He told himself he was using the car for cover, but Scotty knew he had collapsed. He was thankful for the rest the bumper provided as he continued shooting. He could hear the suspect's bullets hitting the rear of the car and going over Scotty's head. *He's shooting quickly,* Scotty thought, *and he can't reload with one hand.* Scotty continued to fire as he waited for the suspect to drop the officer and reach for another magazine on the officer's belt.

Scotty was certain other units were coming, but he could hear nothing. Even his own gun was quiet. All he could hear was the clicking of the firing pin and the movement of the slide. After falling against the car, he started to hear his expended brass dance on the trunk of the suspect's car. *Focus!* he thought. *Stay in the fight!* Scotty knew he had fourteen rounds to stop this guy, but he had no idea of the number of shots he'd fired. In his mind, he knew he was nearing the end of his magazine and the shots to the suspect's chest seemed to have no effect. "Was he wearing body armor?" Scotty said to himself. Then he recalled his training and aimed the next shot carefully at the suspect's right hip.

The bullet landed with a thud, and the suspect went down hard. He also let go of the officer. For the first time since he first observed the suspect, Scotty knew that he could be stopped. When the suspect hit the ground, Scotty saw he still had the gun in his right hand. He watched the suspect in slow motion as he bounced on the ground and immediately picked up his head. Scotty saw the suspect try to roll to find Scotty as he swung his right hand around in his direction. Scotty took an extra microsecond to aim and put a bullet into the suspect's right cheek. The blood spray on the front grill of the patrol car told Scotty he had hit his mark.

As Scotty grabbed a fresh magazine to put into his Glock, he noticed that it felt slick. He put the magazine into the well of the pistol and took a deep breath. Scotty started to get up to check on the officer, who was still not moving, but he was unable to stand. As he looked down at his left leg, he could see a small hole in the front of his uniform pants. However, what he felt behind his left leg was worse; it was a hole the size of a silver dollar, and it was pouring out blood. Scotty had to get to the officer. *He may need CPR,* he thought. When he stumbled again, he nearly said out loud, "I'm gonna need CPR soon if someone doesn't get here!"

As he covered the suspect with his Glock, he began to low crawl to the officer. He swept the gun from the suspect's hand and looked at his face. The suspect was dead. That was obvious. What had once been a human being capable of such good had ceased to exist and now lay bloody on the shoulder of a highway after trying to kill two officers—two strangers he never met who would have responded to his calls for help without hesitation if he called 911.

Scotty's perceptions started to return to normal, and he heard sirens. He also heard someone speaking in front of him. It was the officer's radio. Scotty crawled to it and pushed the emergency button. He holstered his Glock, took a deep breath, and keyed up the microphone. For a moment, he could not speak. The breath he took burned. He focused on staying as calm as he could. He remembered the words he heard in the police academy so many years ago. "If they can't understand you, they can't help you." Scotty released the mic, focused, and then he keyed it up again. His voice was calm and even, but sounded weak.

"Cruiser Two to radio. I need EMS times two." He took another deep breath. "Suspect is down. Officer is down and unconscious. Scene is secure. Start a crime scene unit and homicide."

"Roger Cruiser Two. EMS is en route." The voice on the radio paused, then asked, "Are you Code 4?"

The question somehow struck him by surprise. It was a normal question and reasonable. "Code 4" meant "Are you OK?" He didn't know what to say. He knew he was hurt, but he felt no pain. Adrenaline was the captain of the ship now. He remembered stories of soldiers who said they would have time to be in pain later, when they were safe. He keyed up the mic and spoke as calmly as he could.

"Negative, Radio." Another deep and burning breath. "Cruiser Two is Signal 50. Multiple." His voice started to trail off. He looked down at the officer's name tag and saw blood on his uniform. He quickly scanned the officer for an injury but saw none. Then Scotty wiped his chin.

It was his blood he saw, bright red and frothy, splattering on the young officer's shirt as he spoke. "Lung shot. That's bad," Scotty said out loud. He leaned over to speak into the officer's ear.

"Hang on, Driscoll! Help is on the way."

Scotty saw that the officer was breathing but still unconscious. He heard the officer's radio loudly bark.

"Unit 3037 out with Cruiser Two."

"Unit 3130 out." The radio erupted with a seemingly endless stream of excited voices.

"Radio get EMS in here!" Shouted one officer as he approached Scotty. Scotty recognized the voice. It was John Mander. Scotty was present for his final interview when he was hired on. He was a three-year veteran of the department and a combat medic in the Army Reserve with more than one Bronze Star for bravery under fire. Scotty felt a sense of comfort that Mander was there.

Scotty looked up as Mander handcuffed the suspect. *That's it*, Scotty thought. *Secure the scene.* Scotty realized that Mander hadn't watched the suspect go down. He had to secure him. As John Mander kneeled down next to Scotty, he took charge and started yelling to responding units who were arriving on the scene.

"I need a trauma kit!" He looked at Scotty and spoke again. "Get a defibrillator too."

Scotty looked up at Mander and smiled. He drew in another deep, burning breath and coughed out words to Mander. "What took you so long?" His voice was weak and hardly seemed recognizable. Scotty knew every officer needs to stay calm to function. If he could say something to Mander, he could help him focus.

"I stopped for coffee on the way, Chief. You know you should never get into a gunfight after rush hour!"

That was funny. Scotty tried to laugh, but his chest felt heavy. He coughed and saw more bright pink blood come out. Mander turned his head instinctively.

"Sorry," Scotty said.

"That's OK, Chief. I need you to stay in the fight!"

"Roger that." Scotty could only get two words out between short breaths and coughs. "How's Driscoll?"

"He's breathing but still out."

"Help him," Scotty pushed out. "First."

"We've got him, Chief. His airway's open. Let's focus on you right now." Scotty saw another officer holding both sides of Driscoll's cheeks to keep his airway open while speaking to him.

Scotty realized his eyes were closing. *That's dumb,* he thought. *These folks came to help me, and I'm not even looking them in the eye!* Scotty opened his eyes and what he saw was at once comforting and shocking.

They were all around. Some standing, some kneeling next to him, and others talking into their radios and yelling. There were officers from surrounding departments, at least twenty of them that he could count. He saw uniforms and faces and thought he recognized some of them. As paramedics and firefighters approached him, Scotty heard someone speak.

"Aren't you too old to be making traffic stops?" It was Ronald Parker, the colonel in charge of the state patrol. Scotty had gone to the FBI National Academy with Ronald. He was kneeling on Scotty's left side holding his left hand. Scotty could see that but could hardly feel it.

"Seemed like a good idea at the time," Scotty said, coughing. "Kind of wondering about it now, though." The colonel laughed. Scotty could see that Parker was trying to distract him from the work of the rescuers.

"I can't wait to see the video. Old age and treachery, huh, Scotty?" It was a reference to an old joke between them. It was a saying they'd learned from an old firearms instructor. "Old age and treachery will outperform youth and skill every time."

"Keep quiet, sir. You need your strength." He turned his head. "Give me that O2!" Mander shouted to an EMT. Mander's uniform bore the caduceus, letting the EMTs and firefighters know that he was also a paramedic. Mander used scissors to cut the right side of Scotty's uniform shirt. He also cut through the straps that held his body armor. He palpated Scotty's ribs and held his finger in place. With his right hand, he pulled a scalpel from his personal medic kit. "Hold still, sir. This is going to hurt." Mander pressed the blade against Scotty's skin and made an incision between two ribs.

Scotty winced. He wasn't kidding. It hurt.

"When I say three, sir, take a deep breath in."

"Hey! You can't put in a chest tube!" shouted one of the paramedics who was running up.

"Arrest me!" Mander said. "I've put in more of these than the ER docs at General." He was telling the truth, but the paramedic was right. The insertion of a chest tube was beyond the scope of his civilian paramedic license, but to Mander, this was a battle zone and another hero was losing his grip on life.

Mander held the tube and counted, "One, two, three!"

As Scotty struggled to breathe in, Mander inserted the chest tube and blood shot out of Scotty's chest cavity. The pain was unbelievable, but it suddenly became easier to breath.

"Good job, sir. We'll get you to the ER in no time." Scotty suddenly became aware of his pants being cut off. He also felt someone pressing on his leg to stop the bleeding. Why hadn't he felt that before?

"The oxygen will help, sir. Breathe as deep as you can. Let's get him on a board. Load and go!" Mander said to a police lieutenant. "We need units to escort the ambulance! He's critical. No time to wait for a chopper! We've got to go!"

As Scotty was placed on the backboard and put onto the stretcher, he suddenly felt cold. *It's July. Why do I feel cold?* he thought. That's when he started to realize how badly he was hurt. He looked to the side as he was being placed into the ambulance. For the first time, he saw the spot where he had been lying next to Driscoll. "That's a lot of blood," Scotty said, but no one could hear him. The oxygen mask covered his nose and mouth, and he wasn't even sure he was making any noise anyway. He looked at Ronald, who was in the ambulance with him, along with Mander.

"Stay in the fight, sir! We need you with us!" Scotty saw tears in the eyes of both men. He also saw the paramedic assigned to the ambulance who was working furiously to insert IV lines. Scotty heard him speaking to the doctors at the hospital on the radio. His face looked pale.

Chapter X
Peacemaking

S cotty woke from his deep sleep. Christ was sitting next to him. As Scotty opened his eyes, Christ smiled at him. For the first time since he had arrived, wherever he was, Scotty felt his heart pounding.

"It's not easy being a peacemaker. That's why they need our prayers." Christ said softly.

"That was awful."

"You're OK now."

"Is Driscoll OK?" Scotty realized that the question confirmed for him that he knew this was not a dream.

"His neck is sore, but you interrupted before his windpipe was crushed."

Scotty nodded. "Who was that guy?"

"Jeffrey Bazer. He had just gotten out of prison the day before. He stole that car and was looking for his ex-wife and his lawyer. He was in a blind rage, Scotty. He was ready to kill anyone who stood in his way."

"So Driscoll had no idea?"

"None. He stopped him for speeding. Bazer jumped out of the car right away and met Driscoll at the rear of the car. He knew that if Driscoll approached the car, he would see the damaged steering column. He had decided to kill Driscoll when he first saw the blue lights."

Scotty pondered the words he heard. He thought about the sheer terror Driscoll must have felt. He wondered if Driscoll heard the radio when Scotty said he was there to help. Did he know help was coming, or did he pass out with fear in his heart and without hope?

"He knew, Scotty. He heard you on the radio. He tried to stay conscious until you got there, but Bazer's grip was too strong."

"I'm glad he's OK. I think he got married last year."

"He did. His wife is expecting."

"That's awesome." Scotty paused. "I hope he doesn't quit the department. That guy would have taken nearly anyone down. He didn't do anything wrong."

Christ waited a moment until Scotty was done. He looked at Scotty and locked eyes with him. "You saved his life, Scotty."

Scotty immediately looked down.

"You asked me if you wasted the gifts God gave you, Scotty. You wanted to know if you did enough to help others. Driscoll's little girl will grow up with a daddy because of you."

The words were hard to absorb. "A little girl. Do they know?"

"Well, no, so let's keep that quiet." Christ winked at Scotty. Scotty smiled.

"Driscoll is already using the Cop to Cop program you created. A peer counselor met with him at the hospital."

Scotty looked down. He had started the Cop to Cop program after his meeting with Reggie Pelletier.

"I hoped that would happen." Scotty sighed. "There's so much tied up with cops getting hurt on the job or shooting someone. They get angry at the circumstances, they withdraw, and neither emotion is healthy."

"You changed that, Scotty. That program helped a lot of people."

"It spread to other departments." Scotty paused. "I'm very proud of that."

"You should be."

The two sat in silence, then Christ spoke.

"Why do you think that is, Scotty?"

"The anger and withdrawal?"

"Yes."

"Well, you have to like people to be a cop. If you don't, you won't last long. The things people do to each other and the way some of them speak to and about cops will get to you. I think cops get through being cursed at and beaten up in the press by falling back on the good times with people. We get to see great things, even though they seem small: directing traffic at high school graduations and seeing all of those proud families, responding to calls for lost kids and reuniting them with their parents, helping an older person find their car in a parking lot, and playing ball with kids on duty. That's all good and those memories keep you going. But when you get hurt, or, worse, when you are forced to take a life to save your own or someone else's, it's easy to start thinking there's no more good in the world."

"They have support, though."

"Oh, yes. The department and the community will support them, but this is different. It comes from within. It's like a type of self-doubt."

"Keep going." Christ was leaning towards Scotty now, hanging on every word.

"It can be hard to be a law enforcement officer, but you keep going because you know, or at least you convince yourself that what you've learned growing up is true: If you do the right thing, you will be OK."

Christ nodded his head. "Sometimes doing everything right doesn't mean everything will be all right."

"I've heard that so many times."

"I know." Christ smiled.

"I know that going from a normal patrol shift to facing death eye-to-eye can change things for even the most optimistic officer. I was determined to make sure that if a cop left the job after an assault or a shooting, it was because they wanted to, not because they had to."

"It is a great program. It helped a lot of people." Christ touched Scotty's arm. "It helped you."

Scotty took a deep breath and caught the lump in his throat. It always happened when he thought about the Cop to Cop program. He never wanted the recognition and awards he received for the program. His standard acceptance speech was "It's not about me."

"That's how I got through it and back on the street." Then Scotty smiled and laughed a little.

"What?" Christ was smiling too.

"I always remember the people who thought the program was intended to help cops lie or get their stories straight after a shooting. Part of me wanted to have them sit in on some of those sessions to really see how vulnerable and human we are."

"It's hard for people to understand that, Scotty."

"Why?"

"Everyone, even the people who seem to hate officers, expects that they will be there for them and their families when no one else will be. Most people openly respect those who help others and who sacrifice for strangers."

"I always believed that." Scotty paused at another past-tense reference to his own life.

"No one wants to see their heroes as fallible, vulnerable, or weak. People need to see their protectors as strong. 'We who are strong have an obligation to bear with the failings of the weak, and not to please ourselves. Let each of us please his neighbor for his good, to build him up.' Everyone expects self-sacrifice from officers, and they expect that those sacrifices will be deep, but part of every person wants the people they rely upon to be invincible."

Scotty nodded his head.

"It's why a little boy grows up thinking his dad knows everything and why all comic book heroes have super-powers. That's also why it was important for me to make certain that the things I did on Earth were remembered and written down."

Scotty's forehead wrinkled up and he stared at Christ. "I do not understand."

Christ sat back as he spoke. "My death was and is hard for people to understand. They say, 'How could he be the son of God and not save himself?' I understand why that is so difficult for people. So, people had to hear the stories of what I did on Earth to understand that my death was not a part of my life—it was part of your lives."

"You died for us."

"Willingly, Scotty."

"I remember as a boy being awestruck at your state-ment that God would have sent twelve legions of angels to save you if you asked." Scotty laughed. "I asked my Sunday school teacher how many that was and he said, 'Well, it's a bunch!' "

Christ laughed, and both men looked at each other like old friends recalling a vivid memory.

"He was a good man, Scotty, but that is a tough question and nearly every child wonders that in Sunday school. I bet that question has been asked millions of times when they study the Book of Matthew. He was right, though—it is a bunch!"

Scotty wiped a tear away from his eye. He wasn't sure if it was the laughing or the memory of those awkward and precious times as a child when the world seemed so full of questions. Maybe it was a bit of both.

Christ looked up and thought for a moment. "Cops have to live their lives backwards, in a way. They make their sacrifices and perform miracles but have no idea when either will occur. Many times, the miracles are known to no one."

"Cops performing miracles?"

"Oh yes, Scotty. The DUI driver who spends the night in jail but does not kill the nurse on her way home from work, the fourteen-year-old who spends a lot of time talking to an officer on the way to jail from a shoplifting arrest who decides to turn his life around, and the rapist who leaves the area because he sees a patrol car in the neighborhood. Those are all miracles in their own right."

"I never looked at things that way."

"It's not just public servants, Scotty. Some people perform miracles evidencing the love of God every day they walk, help a stranger, or raise a child."

"So how do cops do it backwards?"

"I knew the plan for my time on Earth. I knew my sacrifice would come at the end of my life, and I knew the miracles I had to perform to allow people to see. Remember John's words, Scotty: 'Jesus did many other things as well. If every one of them was written down, I suppose that even the whole world would not have room for the books that would be written.' I was on Earth to fulfill a purpose that was known to me."

"That still could not have made your life easy."

"Not easy, Scotty, but a life of service is never easy. My point is that officers have no idea what plans are made for them, and many times, their sacrifices come at the beginning of their lives. Only through their faith and the faith of those they leave behind can people truly understand that their heroes are human."

After a while, Scotty got up and began walking around.

"The bullet wounds, that's what I've been feeling."

"Yes."

Scotty shook his head then was quiet for a while. "Who told Celina?"

"Bob Shoop sent an officer to pick her up. He called her first."

"Is she OK?"

"She's scared. She's been with you since she got to the hospital."

"How long?"

"Two weeks."

Scotty's heart sank. "That's awful. I sat by Christine's bed and my parents' beds, waiting. That's no way to live." Scotty was choked up with tears filling his eyes.

"I can fight as long as I need to, but she deserves a better life than watching me. I don't want that for her. She went through enough losing her mother."

"She's strong, Scotty. She can get through this." Christ paused and looked up at Scotty. "But what do you want?"

The words struck Scotty off-guard. "What do you mean?"

"You're thinking about Celina, Scotty. You have thought of her first since the day she was born. What do you want?"

The words were hard to hear. There were so many questions. A few moments ago, or so it seemed, there was so much time to think and ask and ponder the answers. Now his mind was spinning like a top. What did Christ mean? He was always told there is a plan for everyone. Did he really get to choose? If he did, how could he leave Celina? She meant everything to him.

For the first time, Scotty started to see the rich colors of a sunset forming. It was the most beautiful sunset he'd ever felt. He knew he could only see the colors, but still he felt this sunset. The sun approaching the horizon seemed to move closer as it approached. He was lost in the way a person loses sight of everything else the first time they see true beauty.

"Is that it? Is this where I stand? A choice between leaving my daughter or letting her watch me suffer?"

Christ just looked at Scotty. Even now, just the sight of him provided comfort. Scotty took a moment before he spoke.

"I have to know something. You've told me that people make choices; sometimes they make bad choices. But I need to know something. You've told me so much, but I cannot tell you what I want until I know more."

There was silence between them. For the first time, Scotty felt uncomfortable with the passage of time. Then Christ spoke.

"You will not survive, Scotty. The bullets did too much damage." Christ paused. "Your body is strong from working out, but some things cannot be fixed."

"Why have I survived this long?"

"Your will to live, Scotty. You're a fighter. You always have been. Without it, you would not have lived to see the ambulance arrive."

"How long?" Scotty said nearly in a whisper.

"No more than ten days, but you will not regain consciousness. How long is up to you, Scotty, and how hard you fight."

"But you can fix this! You brought people back from the dead, I believe that. Forget about me—so many people will suffer if I die. My daughter will lose her father!"

"Some things must be, Scotty. People are formed by the good and bad in their lives. You became the man you are because you lost your dad at nine years old, and Celina will grow in her own life because of this. The people around you will be changed not only by your passing, but by the time they spent with you. Your heroic acts and sacrifice will drive them, and they will save the lives of others."

"I'll never get to say goodbye to Celina?" His voice trailed off.

Christ stood and put his hand on Scotty's shoulder.

"How will she get past this?"

"The same way you moved past the painful times in your life. All God's children have an incredible ability to move past hardship and sorrow. True, it shapes them, but that is part of who they are. Do you remember the days after your father's funeral?"

"Yes. I'll never forget them."

"Those were hard days, Scotty. What was the hardest part for you?"

"The mornings. We would spend time together before he went to work. He would come in and wake me up. He called it our 'morning meeting.'" Scotty looked down.

"What did you talk about?"

"His day, my day, school, superheroes, anything really."

"Those first few days were the toughest, Scotty, but you learned to fill those times that you missed him."

"I did, but I felt guilty."

"Why did you feel guilty?"

Scotty's eyes began to tear. As he spoke, a tear ran down his left cheek. "I was afraid that if I moved on, I would forget him."

Christ allowed some time to pass before he spoke.

"We never forget the ones we love, Scotty. Parts of our memories may fade with time, but that's not what they meant to us. The essence of them, their warmth, the way they made us feel, those things are embedded within us. You see Scotty, the people we love change us and always for the better. Like a stream that carries minerals as it flows, we pick up parts of other people throughout our lives. The journey is richer because of the people we meet and more so for the people we love."

"I still think about my dad. I know he would be proud of me."

"Yes, Scotty, he would. You are the man you are because you were loved by him. Imagine if everyone in the world truly understood the power of God's love. If they only realized how much it can transform them into something wonderful. Remember, Scotty, love is a two-way proposition. You could not have benefitted from your father's love if you did not love him, and you loved him very much."

"Yes, I did. As much as I didn't think it was possible, I have always loved Celina more."

"Of course, Scotty. We are meant to love our children more than life itself."

Scotty looked at Christ. "I always did and she always loved me more than I ever dreamed possible. I saw that love grow when we lost Christine. I didn't think that was possible, but it did for both of us."

"That's how both of you survived that loss, Scotty. You and Christine also taught her to love, and she has loved many people. Because of that, she is loved by many." Christ pulled Scotty close. "She will never be alone, Scotty. You will always be with her."

Scotty knew there was no answer. He'd learned that much. The answers were within him his whole life. He looked at Christ and knew in his heart what he had to do.

Chapter XI
No Easy Choices

The hospital room was filled with people. There were homicide detectives on constant vigil to hear anything from Scotty's lips, and friends who cycled in and out, despite warnings from hospital staff. On the streets in the city, officers worked their beats, detectives interviewed victims, deputies served warrants, and the business of law enforcement moved forward as everyone waited for word about Deputy Chief Scotty Painter.

The doctors and nurses who pushed themselves to the limit of their knowledge and abilities to keep him alive were buzzing in and out of the room. Of course, there was Celina. She was sitting by his bed, as she'd been for nearly every minute since arriving at the hospital.

"We can only wait," the neurosurgeon said to Celina. "Time will tell us, but he was badly injured."

She heard these words from the trauma surgeon as well, and the pulmonologist and the nephrologist when she gave the consent to start dialysis after Scotty's kidneys stopped functioning normally.

"You're still not sure he can hear me? I talk to him all the time."

"No one really knows. His brain function is still active, but we know so little about the perception of people in a coma."

Celina dropped her head.

The doctor touched her arm. "I would talk to him too if he were my dad."

Celina picked up her head and looked at Scotty. She had seen that same blank expression for two weeks now. Then something happened. The doctor saw it too.

"Talk to him! Say something!"

"Daddy, it's me! Can you hear me? Can you open your eyes?"

Everyone saw the twitch in his right eyelid. They were all staring intently at his face. His left eyelid began to clench. Then, after what seemed like an hour, both eyes opened.

"Mr. Painter, can you see me?" The doctor took out his penlight and shined it briefly in Scotty's eyes. "Don't try to talk. You have a breathing tube in your throat."

Scotty looked at the people in the room. They were fuzzy and unclear. He felt someone move to his left and push against him on the bed. He could not move his head, but he saw a face come into his field of vision. It was Celina. Her face was not fuzzy at all. It was clear and beautiful.

Scotty saw the tears streaming down her face. People were talking to him, but he could hear only Celina's voice.

"Can you see me? I've got you! I'm holding on!"

All at once, Scotty felt her hand tightly gripping his left hand. Through the fog of the pain and confusion, he focused on her warm hand in his. He was at once aware that more people were coming into the room, but he focused on Celina. He tried to smile at her, but the tube made that impossible.

Scotty felt the machine filling his lungs with air as he lay there. In the confusion of the movement all around him, lights shining in his eyes, nurses adjusting the monitors, Scotty saw only Celina and felt only her hand. His eyes teared as he watched her, exhausted and all at once panicked and excited. As a tear from his left eye ran down his cheek, Scotty gathered all the strength that was in him. He squeezed Celina's hand twice as fast as he could.

Then he was gone.

Chapter XII

As Time Moves Forward

The sun reflected off the bright silver and gold badges in the crowd. Hundreds of officers, deputies, troopers, marshals, and special agents stood at attention on the finely manicured lawn as seven honor guard members fired their rifles. They worked the actions then fired again. They worked the actions again and fired one last time. The crowd was silent as the distant clicking began. It became louder as the roar of the engines came into focus. Tears filled the eyes of everyone assembled as five law enforcement helicopters appeared on the horizon. As they approached, the sound became deafening. They were low and flying slowly in a V-formation. As they were nearly over the cemetery, one of the helicopters peeled off quickly from the formation. The remaining aircraft continued over the crowd.

As quiet seemed to settle on the crowd, a single bugle sounded the first note of "Taps." A bugler at the other side of the crowd answered, and the two continued until they were through. When they finished, the sound of hooves on pavement broke the silence as the horses from the caisson that carried Scotty Painter's body walked down the long path toward the cemetery entrance. The distinctive sound was disturbed only by the occasional sniffle from those assembled. It was a memory that would stay with everyone for the rest of their lives. The empty wagon was a poignant reminder of the life that had ended, the weight of the loss that required so many strong and noble animals to carry it, and the knowledge that far too soon, the wagon would again be filled with the body of a valiant warrior who'd traded another life for the safety of strangers.

Under a tent at the grave, Celina and her husband stood with Bob Shoop, Ronald Parker, and John Mander. Mander, who had attended the funerals of more soldiers than he cared to remember, looked pale and weak. He had insisted on standing guard at the funeral home over Scotty's body. It was a law enforcement tradition that a fallen officer is never left alone until he is buried.

As the last tones of the bugles faded, Bob Shoop hugged Celina. As their embrace ended, she looked over his shoulder to see a seemingly endless line of uniforms waiting to hug her, show their respect, and offer their support. She had known many of them from the time she was a little girl. She had met others during the three days of visitation at the funeral home.

Next in line were Evan Driscoll and his wife, Susan. Evan's neck was still badly bruised and he was unable to wear the tie that went with his dress uniform. As they looked at each other, they began to cry. No words were necessary. They hugged for what seemed like an hour while the rest of the line waited patiently.

Through the hugs and tears, Celina nearly became numb. Many of the older cops approached and kissed her forehead as they hugged her. It was like she was a little girl coming to the precinct again with her daddy after preschool to pick up a case file or a paycheck.

As she stood there, she saw uniforms from all over. Most she recognized, as they were from all over the state and surrounding states. She broke the embrace of a woman she did not know when all at once, five officers approached her and stood at attention. The line of people and those standing around stopped as all five saluted her. They were wearing bright dress uniforms she had never seen before. The crowd was silent as a lieutenant stepped forward.

"My name is Lieutenant John Sanda. This is the honor guard from my department. Your father saved my life when I was a boy." He stopped and swallowed choking back his emotions, but he never broke eye contact with Celina. "My sister, my mother, and I are alive because of his bravery and dedication." He looked to his left and nodded. A corporal reached under his left arm and removed a tightly folded flag. He handed it to Lieutenant Sanda.

"This is the flag of my department. Yesterday, it flew over our state capitol. The day before that, it flew over our department. I am honored to present it to you." He stepped forward, handed the flag to Celina, then stepped back and saluted again slowly. Then, in unison, the five officers turned and walked away. The crowd was speechless. As they turned, Colonel Parker looked at their shoulder patches and whispered to Celina.

"Colonial County, Colorado. That's a long way. Do you know the connection to your dad?"

"No, but that's OK. He knows, and I know he's watching."

Celina's husband held the folded American flag presented to Celina by the Governor herself. Celina wore the department's highest award, the Medal of Valor, around her neck. Bob Shoop had presented the medal to her at the funeral. He told the crowd it was the last gesture of thanks to her father from a grateful community. He called Scotty Painter a "true hero who served with honor." Celina knew her dad would have been proud and humbled by the funeral service.

Celina wanted to crumble, but she had to be strong. She was a cop's daughter. Her dad had died a hero, and she would make him proud today and for the rest of her life. She knew, somehow, that he would always be with her.

On the beach, with a light breeze blowing, Scotty Painter saw someone approaching. It was too far away to focus on the face, but he knew instantly who it was. He had waited five long years to see her again. She was not alone, and he recognized the endless, playful game of tag between Fritz and Mr. Biscuit. The two old friends were reunited.

Far from the last time he gazed upon Christine, they had all the time in the world to be together now. He knew he would never let her go.

About the Author

L ance LoRusso is a law enforcement officer turned attorney. Having worked as a street cop, trainer, hostage negotiator, public relations officer, and investigator, he regularly trains law enforcement officers from around the United States. As an attorney, he responds to the scene of officer involved shootings and represents officers through interviews with homicide and internal affairs investigators as well as grand jury hearings. His book, *When Cops Kill: The Aftermath of a Critical Incident,* explores all aspects of an officer involved shooting, including the media scrutiny, investigations, civil suits, and living with having taken a life in the line of duty. The book includes interviews from officers who used deadly force, officers who were shot in the line of duty, and family members who received the call they dreaded. The book is used in law enforcement academies, advanced training for law enforcement executives, and college courses in criminal justice. All of the profits from *When Cops Kill* support law enforcement charities like www.huntingforheroes.org. Lance LoRusso practices law in Atlanta, Georgia, where he lives with his wife, Barbara.

Books by Lance LoRusso

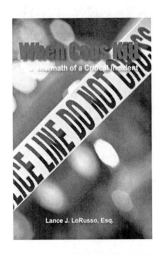

When Cops Kill
The Aftermath of a Critical Incident

The World Class Rainmaker:
Raising the Bar in Your Law Practice